★ SADDLES, STARS, & STRIPES ★

RIDING THE PONY EXPRESS

From the battlegrounds of the Civil War to the California goldfields, the Saddles, Stars, & Stripes series sweeps you back through American history on an unforgettable journey. Each story's very special heroine comes from a different time and culture, but all share a great love of horses and a unique brand of courage.

★   ★   ★

KINGFISHER
a Houghton Mifflin Company imprint
222 Berkeley Street
Boston, Massachusetts 02116
www.houghtonmifflinbooks.com

First published in 2006
2 4 6 8 10 9 7 5 3 1

LIBRARY OF CONGRESS CATALOGING-IN-PUBLICATION DATA
has been applied for.

ISBN 0-7534-6001-7
ISBN 978-07534-6001-6

Printed in India
1TR/0106/THOM/MA/80SSH/C

★ SADDLES, STARS, & STRIPES ★

RIDING THE PONY EXPRESS

DEBORAH KENT

KINGFISHER

BOSTON

✳ Chapter One ✳

"I will lift up mine eyes unto the hills, from whence cometh my help," intoned Reverend Harkness. "My help cometh from the Lord, who made the heaven and the earth . . ."

Lexie McDonald gazed at the ring of peaks looming above her. *Reverend Harkness can talk all he wants,* she thought, *but there is no help from the hills today.* The reverend's words rattled around her, as dry and lifeless as kindling.

A gust of wind whipped through the crowd of mourners. Mrs. Harkness clapped one hand onto her bonnet and tried to hold it in place, all the time looking solemn and proper, as if nothing was amiss. For an instant, Lexie thought of turning to Papa with raised eyebrows, sharing a bemused moment. Not even the Wyoming wind could ruffle the dignity of Mrs. Harkness.

In the next instant the truth crashed in on her again, as it had a thousand times over the past two days. Papa wasn't standing beside her. She would never see him again. Reverend Harkness was performing the funeral service beside Papa's newly dug grave.

Even now she couldn't quite believe that Papa lay sleeping in that narrow pine box that Will Jenkins had hammered together yesterday morning. All of these people—the whole town of Willow Springs, in fact—had gathered for his funeral, yet to Lexie nothing felt real. At any moment she expected Papa to step up beside her with a mischievous grin and beckon her to follow him. She'd slip away, right from under the watchful eyes of Mrs. Harkness, and laugh with him about how he'd fooled everyone into thinking he was dead and gone. "They can't get rid of me that easy!" he'd say. "Not a tough old guy like me!"

"Now let us repeat the Lord's Prayer," Reverend Harkness said. Lexie folded her hands and added her voice to the murmur around her. The familiar words caught in her throat, and she fell silent by the time they came to "forgive us our trespasses." *I'm not going to cry,* she told herself fiercely. *Not now, in front of all these people! Papa would want me to be strong!*

The prayer came to an end. Reverend Harkness uttered some phrases about "ashes to ashes, dust to dust," and the first handfuls of earth thudded onto the lid of the coffin. Mrs. Harkness turned to Lexie. "Come on, dear," she said in a low voice. "We'll all go back to the parsonage for a little something to eat."

Food was the last thing on Lexie's mind. Nothing could comfort her but a long ride on her buckskin gelding, Cougar. "I'm really not hungry, thank you," she said. "I'd like to be by myself for a while."

Mrs. Harkness clicked her tongue and frowned. "All these people came to pay their respects to your father," she said. "It's your duty to show some appreciation."

Already, Lexie was learning that she couldn't argue when Mrs. Harkness had made up her mind. "Yes, I know," she said. "I'm grateful that everyone came. I really am."

It was wonderful to see that so many people cared about her father, Lexie reflected as she followed Mrs. Harkness along Main Street. Over and over, people had told her how much they would miss him, and they meant what they said. The Scotsman Rob McDonald had been a mainstay in the community. For ten years he'd run the general store, selling nails, twine, feed, sugar, and salt to the settlers for 20 miles around. During the past year he'd been a stationmaster for the Russell, Majors, and Waddell company that ran the Pony Express—the company was determined to provide the most reliable mail service available, and Papa had respected their strict ethical values. The Pony Express was about good men providing the best service possible—through rain, snow, sleet, and hail—and Papa had admired their determination.

As the Willow Springs stationmaster, stabling horses and readying them for each relay rider who galloped in, Papa was known for almost 50 miles up the trail east and west for his good humor, his fairness, and his honesty. It became one of Papa's passions that, one day, the Pony Express would become the official mail carrier for the United States, and so he dutifully played his part in getting the mail delivered ·on time. No wonder so many people had put aside their work and come to say their last good-byes.

"I suppose you'll want to get the rest of your things

from the station," Mrs. Harkness said as they walked along. "Some little keepsakes for your new room."

"I'll ride over there later," Lexie said. "But I won't be staying long at the parsonage."

Mrs. Harkness eyed her doubtfully. "It could be weeks till we hear from your aunt back east. And if the snow comes early and the passes are closed, you might be with us till next spring."

"It's very kind of you to have me," Lexie said. The reverend and his wife meant well, but Lexie couldn't imagine staying with them all winter long! Just another three days under their roof would drive her crazy—and moving to New York City, a place she'd never been, to live with an aunt she'd never met would be much worse. She couldn't let them send her east; somehow she had to think of a way out!

At the little clapboard house that Willow Springs called the parsonage people were already gathering. A few neighbor women were in the kitchen, loading platters with bread and meat and pies. They greeted Lexie sympathetically and urged her to eat, but she thanked them and shook her head. "Go and sit in the parlor," Mrs. Harkness told her. "People will want to offer their condolences."

Slowly, her feet as heavy as stone, Lexie left the kitchen. She didn't know what to say to all those sorry, somber people. She wasn't sure she could answer them without bursting into tears. She paused outside the kitchen door, bracing herself for the ordeal ahead, when behind her she heard one of the women say, "He was such a fine man! So hardworking and steady!"

Lexie lingered to listen. She treasured every word in praise of her father. In some small way those kind remembrances brought him back to her. "He took sick so suddenly!" Lexie recognized the nervous, fluttery voice of May Jenkins, the carpenter's wife. "Tuesday I heard he was down with a pain in his belly, and Wednesday he was gone."

"My husband says it was the trouble over Callum that killed him," said Mrs. Harkness. "That boy broke his father's heart. But the traits were there; they were bound to come out."

Lexie tensed as she listened.

"Alexandra, she's different," May Jenkins said. "She's as pretty as any white girl. You'd hardly guess—"

"It shows a bit in her face," Mrs. Harkness said. "And the straight black hair, of course. But mostly she takes after her father, thank heavens!"

"That boy," May Jenkins said with a sigh. "The first

time I saw him I took him for a full-blooded Indian!"

"They couldn't keep him in school, you know," another voice chimed in. "Any chance he got he was out the door, riding off to who knows where on some half-wild bronco."

"I wasn't surprised when I heard about the business with the mail pouch," May Jenkins said. "What else can you expect?"

"He'll hang if they ever catch him," Mrs. Harkness said with a hint of satisfaction. "But don't tar Alexandra with the same brush. Once she settles down, she'll be a proper young lady."

Lexie's stomach lurched. She had heard more than enough. She couldn't bear to spend another moment at the parsonage now. Without a word to anyone, she slipped through the back door and dashed to the field behind the house.

The wind had risen, and the late summer air was crisp and cool. Trying to steady herself, Lexie breathed in the familiar smells of hay and wildflowers. She hadn't cried at the funeral, but now, at last, her eyes burned with tears. How dare they speak like that about Callum on the same day as Papa's funeral! Nothing could hurt Papa more than cruel words about his son. And how dare they talk about Indian blood as though it was a curse. "As pretty as any white girl!" she repeated, almost choking on the words. "I don't want to be like any white girl!" she cried. "Not if it means growing up to be like them."

Not far from the barn, Mrs. Harkness' chestnut mare, Hattie, grazed quietly. Cougar was farther off, near a cluster of piñon pines. When Cougar was a colt, Lexie had trained him to come when she gave the lonesome whistle of the mountain quail. It had been a chance to teach him loyalty and obedience, a way to strengthen the bond between them. Now she tilted back her head and gave the quail's low, clear whistle. Cougar lifted his head and trotted toward her with light, eager steps.

Lexie leaned against Cougar's shoulder. He stood still and solid, unshakable in the midst of her turmoil. She slid her arms around his neck and felt his warm, smooth hide against her tear-stained cheek. "Oh, Cougar," she moaned. "I'm an orphan now! What am I going to do?" Cougar twisted his head around to nuzzle her hair. In the only way he could he seemed to be assuring her that everything would be all right.

Lexie had lost all of the people she had ever loved. A sudden, terrible illness had snatched away her father.

Her brother, Callum, had fled town six months ago, accused of stealing a valuable package from the Pony Express mail. Her mother, the woman who gave the McDonald children their Arapaho blood, had died when Lexie was only five. Only Cougar was left, and if the reverend and his wife sent her to Aunt Grace McDonald, Cougar would have to stay behind in Wyoming Territory. She would lose him, too.

By now, Mrs. Harkness had probably noticed that she wasn't sitting in the parlor. They were sure to send someone searching for her. She would have to move fast if she was going to get her ride.

Hurrying to the barn, Lexie lifted Cougar's saddle from the rack. It was a boy's saddle, not a lady's sidesaddle like the one that Mrs. Harkness used for sedate little rides on Hattie. Lexie was still wearing the long, black skirt that Mrs. Harkness had lent her for the funeral. It was completely unsuitable for riding astride. She had made herself a divided skirt that allowed her to ride with almost as much ease and freedom as a boy, but it was still back at the station. It was one of the things that she wanted to collect and bring back to the parsonage.

Lexie hadn't been able to take Cougar out for a run since the day Papa got sick. Now he was "wound tight

13

as a spring," as Papa would say. As Lexie saddled him up, he neighed playfully to Hattie. *It's as if he's telling her he wished she could come along too,* Lexie thought. Cougar had always been friendly with other horses, ready to play whenever he had the chance. Maybe it was because he'd missed out on being with other colts when he was growing up.

Lexie put a foot in the stirrup and flung her other leg across Cougar's back. She gathered the black skirt out of the way as well as she could and picked up the reins. She didn't have to nudge him ahead with her heels. As soon as she was in the saddle, Cougar set off for the hills at a brisk trot.

Three years ago, when she was 12, Lexie had found Cougar in a sagebrush hollow, trembling beside the bloodied body of his mother. Lexie had ridden out that day on Callum's bay gelding, Ranger, to watch the herd of wild mustangs that had been grazing there for weeks. But the herd was gone, all but the spindly-legged buckskin colt and the fallen mare. The colt hadn't wanted to leave his mother, but Lexie coaxed him to follow her back to town, holding out her fingers for him to suck on. He seemed to take comfort from her presence, and from that day on he had been her horse in such a special way. They had each lost their mother when they were very young, and Lexie felt that they shared an invisible bond of understanding.

"Sounds like it was a mountain lion—a cougar— that killed the mare," Papa had said when he saw the colt and heard Lexie's story. "No wonder the rest of the herd ran off."

Lexie had never seen a live cougar, but once a rancher rode into town to collect a bounty on one he'd shot. Draped limply across the rancher's saddle, it was both sinister and beautiful. Its body was lithe and golden, graceful even in death. Its dead claws raked the empty air, and its razor-sharp teeth snarled at the curious crowd.

She was aghast when Callum suggested that she give the name "Cougar" to the colt. "Never!" Lexie exclaimed. "Why should he live with the reminder of what happened? He should have a bright, happy name to help him forget."

Papa shook his head thoughtfully. "Callum has a point," he told her. "This colt got off to a rough start in life. Some horses don't recover from a thing like that. It leaves them skittish, and you can never count on them. Your mother's people say there's power in a name. If you call the colt Cougar, maybe he'll find the strength to get over his fear."

Perhaps the name had worked magic. Cougar was high-spirited, even willful at times, but he wasn't skittish. Once when a jackrabbit leaped up right under his hooves, he hadn't even flinched. He'd grown up to be a horse that she could count on, and he'd become her best friend. Now he was all she had left.

✳ Chapter Two ✳

After his days of inactivity, Lexie thought Cougar would be eager to run. Instead he seemed to sense her need for silence. He slid into a smooth, steady canter that brought her ease and comfort. It gave her time to think.

They left the town behind them and climbed a winding trail that they both knew well. Piñon pines and clumps of sagebrush clung to the rocky mountainside. Newcomers sometimes said that this country had a foreboding look and were frightened by its rugged vastness. To Lexie, the land had a stark, wild beauty. She knew where the Indian paintbrush bloomed each spring and where the blackbirds made their nests. Every rise and hollow, each jutting boulder and twisted pine, spoke to her of home.

It would all be lost to her if she went to live with Aunt Grace in New York City. Papa had lived there long ago, just after he and his family moved to America from Scotland. Papa said the city was always noisy, with carts clattering over the cobblestone streets and vendors shouting. The houses were crowded next to each other as tightly as the needles on a pine branch. "There wasn't much room to breathe," he used to say. "And the wee bit of air we had was full of soot."

Papa left New York at the age of 16 and never went back. He wandered all over the west, trapping beavers and other animals for their furs. One winter, snowbound in the Wind River Mountains, he camped with a band of Arapaho and met Mama. Mama had learned some English from missionaries who had lived in the town years before. They had even given her an English name, Nancy Marie. Papa became fluent in Inuna-Ina, the Arapaho language, and called her by her true name: *Nech Ni'ibei'inaa*—"Water that Sings."

Papa didn't ask Mama to move to a white town, knowing people would always look down on her as an Indian. He stayed with her people for almost 14 years. Then, in the summer of 1850, smallpox swept through the Arapaho village. Papa told Lexie once, "So many people died that the rest of us ran out of tears." Mama died and Lexie's baby sister, Caroline. The best hunters in the town died and even the medicine man. When the chief died, the last survivors scattered and disappeared into the mountains. Papa never learned what became of them. He moved Callum and Lexie to Willow Springs and took over the general store.

Lexie was five when they went to live in Willow Springs. She mastered English right away and soon forgot how to speak her mother tongue. The change was more difficult for Callum, who was 12 that summer. He always spoke English a little haltingly, as though the words didn't come to him with a natural flow. It was true, what that woman said back at the parsonage—Callum couldn't bear to sit in a schoolroom. He had to be outdoors, hunting or fishing or riding a fast horse. It was the Indian in him, people said, and they'd shake their heads knowingly.

Because Lexie had fair skin, she could pass as white, and the people of Willow Springs generally accepted her. But they never fully accepted Callum, with his copper skin and his silent Indian walk, and Callum never quite accepted Willow Springs.

Papa tried to change all that when he urged Callum to sign up as a rider with "the Pony," as the relay mail system was affectionately called. Everyone admired the galloping Pony Express riders who sped the mail back and forth across mountains, plains, and deserts between St. Joseph, Missouri, and California.

Pony Express riders were tough, brave, and determined. They rode day and night, 100 miles or more, only stopping to switch horses at each relay station. They were known to be honest and upstanding young men as well. In order to work for the company, they even had to take an oath promising not to drink, swear, or gamble. "If you become a successful Pony rider," Papa told Callum, "people will see what you're really made of."

Willow Springs was a home station, a place where Pony riders could get a hot meal and a decent rest, as well as a fresh horse. Whenever Callum rode back into Willow Springs, he was bursting with stories for Lexie and Papa. He would tell them how he got caught in a blizzard and only found the next station because his horse knew the way. He talked about friendly rivalries with the other riders, how they tried to shave minutes off their time from one station to the next. For the first time that Lexie could remember, her brother really seemed to be happy. Then, in Callum's third month with the Pony, everything went wrong.

Ordinarily the Pony Express only transported letters—at five dollars an ounce. It was a luxury to send even a lightweight envelope. But there were rich gold miners in California, men who were happy to pay whatever it cost to ship a package with the Pony. One day rumors raced up the trail that the next mochila, or mail pouch, contained something unusually valuable. A mochila was the special carrier that all the Pony riders used. Made of soft, lightweight leather, it consisted of four pouches held together with straps and lacings. It rested neatly over the saddle, one pouch dangling at each corner.

This mochila contained a diamond ring. The ring was a special present destined for the bride of a gold miner in San Francisco. When the mochila with the ring arrived in Willow Springs, it was Callum's turn to carry it westward on the next leg of its journey.

Callum set out, tall and proud in the saddle. Lexie knew it meant a great deal to him that the company trusted him with such a crucial mission. But somehow Callum's mochila never reached Green River, the next home station. Callum swore he'd turned it over to the stationmaster late at night in the midst of a whirling snowstorm. The stationmaster, however, insisted that Callum had never arrived at all that night. One of them had to be lying, people said, and it certainly wasn't the stationmaster! There was a valuable package in the mochila, they said, and that half-breed McDonald boy knew where it was.

The superintendent in charge of the Third Pony Express Division, the trail that stretched from Elkhorn, Wyoming, to Salt Lake City, Utah, was called in to investigate. By the time he arrived, Callum was gone. Lexie knew he'd have been thrown in jail—and probably hanged—if he'd stayed in Willow Springs. No judge in the territory was likely to believe his story. Lexie and Papa were sure that he was innocent. Yet, by running away, Callum confirmed his guilt in the minds of the townspeople.

As Cougar cantered up the trail, Lexie wondered

for the hundredth time where Callum had gone. Perhaps he had set out to find an Arapaho village that would take him in. He might be at peace there, among people who spoke Inuna-Ina and shared his love for life in the open. Was there anyone left who remembered him from the days before Mama died? Did any living soul besides Callum and Lexie still remember their mother, Water that Sings?

The path leveled off, and Cougar loped through a narrow passageway between craggy granite walls. In a few minutes they emerged into a sun-dappled meadow, the tall grass brushing against Cougar's belly and swishing around his legs. Lexie reined him in and gave him time to crop the grass. High above them, a hawk floated in effortless circles. Sometimes, when Callum saw a hawk, he murmured a chant in Inuna-Ina. Lexie couldn't remember the words, but Callum had taught her what it meant. "Look well, hawk in the sky. Watch over the ones I love."

Callum is the only real family I have left, Lexie thought. If she knew where he was right now, no matter how far away, she'd set out on Cougar to find him. When they discussed where she should go after Papa died, Reverend Harkness and his wife had never even considered that she might live with her brother. When they had asked Lexie if Papa had any relatives, they were relieved when she mentioned his sister back east. As far as they were concerned, Aunt Grace in New York City was the answer.

"You're at an age where you need a woman to bring you up," Mrs. Harkness had told her. "You'll be able to wear pretty dresses and white gloves in New York. Won't that be lovely?"

You can't ride horses in pretty dresses and white gloves, Lexie thought. She couldn't imagine a more miserable existence.

Someone must know where Callum was. He couldn't simply vanish like the morning fog. Maybe one of the Pony riders had gotten word of him. Callum had made friends with them, and they had liked him, too. One of them, Billy Cates, had been his special friend. She would find out when Billy was due into the station, Lexie decided. She'd insist that he tell her everything he knew.

By now they had reached the smooth, open meadow where she and Callum used to race, she on Cougar and Callum on Ranger. The ground was so even that the horses could run at top speed without worrying about holes and drop-offs and loose rocks.

"Come on, Cougar!" Lexie cried, picking up the reins. "Now's your chance to gallop!"

Cougar didn't have to be told. He was off the instant that Lexie's heels touched his flanks. Gripping tightly with her knees, Lexie leaned forward along his neck. They sailed across the meadow, as wild and free as the hawk in the sky. Cougar slowed to make his way through the pass between broken boulders, but he gathered speed again as they clattered down the mountain trail. Lexie grabbed his mane with one hand as he jounced over rocks and leaped over a fallen log, never breaking his stride. She was thrilled by his speed and power. She was sure that if Mr. Russell and Mr. Majors and Mr. Waddell ever found out what a fast horse he was, they'd want to buy him for the Pony Express. He'd be great for carrying the mail, she knew, but she would never sell him. Cougar belonged to her.

From long habit, Cougar turned in at the Pony station and came to a snorting halt at the corral gate. Lexie slid off his back and unfastened his saddle. She picked up some handfuls of straw and rubbed him down after his run. Two Pony Express horses were resting in the barn. A third stood in the corral, saddled, bridled, and ready to go when the next rider came in. Cougar whinnied to the strange horse, a nervous little black mare. He tried to touch noses with her, but she bared her teeth and shied away. Cougar bent his head and pulled up a mouthful of grass, as if he didn't mind at all.

Josh Wiggins, who was acting as the stationmaster until the company sent a permanent replacement, hurried out of the cabin. He looked uncomfortable when he recognized Lexie, as though he didn't quite know what to say to her. "How you doing?" he asked. "Funeral went off all right?"

Lexie nodded. She didn't want to think about Papa's funeral just now. "Which riders are due today?" she asked.

Wiggins frowned. "I don't know all their names yet," he admitted. "The westbound fellow should be here any minute now, and the eastbound rider won't be long."

Of course, Josh Wiggins didn't know the riders' names yet. He was brand-new to the Pony. Two days ago he'd been out in the hills herding cattle, and he'd go back to his herd as soon as the official stationmaster arrived. "May I go in and get some clothes I left?" she asked.

"Of course you can!" he exclaimed. "Take anything you need."

Lexie could hardly believe that she had left Willow Springs Station only two days ago. The door gave its familiar creak, and the floorboards still rang hollowly under her feet as she stepped inside. She saw the plank table, lined with rough wooden stools, where she and Papa had eaten their meals with whatever riders were there. The usual fragrance of coffee hung in the air, and as always, a pot of soup steamed on the fire. Nothing had changed, but without Papa, nothing could ever be the same again.

Lexie scrambled up the ladder to the loft that was her room. She had only lived in it for a year, but it still felt like home. It was a small, narrow space beneath the slanting roof, too low to let her stand upright.

Lexie knew exactly what she wanted to get first. Tucked into a corner beneath the eaves lay the little pine box that Callum had given her for her ninth birthday, a special place to store her most cherished keepsakes. Lexie drew it from its hiding place and cradled it lovingly in her hands. She'd have to find somewhere safe for it at the parsonage, she thought. She didn't want Mrs. Harkness peering into it, frowning over her treasures.

Next she pulled a skirt from the walnut chest that

held her clothes and admired it in the hazy light that crept in through the cracks. It was a simple blue calico, spreading wide from a slender waist. Lexie had slit it almost to the top with Papa's shears and had sewn the seams to form a pair of billowing pants. When she stood on the ground, she seemed to be wearing an ordinary skirt.

Outside she heard the pounding of hoofbeats. The westbound rider was in! Lexie slipped gratefully into her riding skirt and hurried back down the ladder. She darted out the door to see who had arrived.

The Pony rider was perched on a pinto mare, its flanks heaving, its hide flecked with sweat. He was small and wiry like most of the Pony riders, but his suntanned face beamed at Lexie with a smile that she would recognize anywhere. She could hardly believe her good fortune. It was Callum's best friend, Billy Cates.

✴ Chapter Three ✴

Billy slid to the ground and leaned against the fence, looking almost as winded as his horse. He'd probably ridden a hundred miles, Lexie thought, stopping for only two or three minutes at the relay stations along the way. No wonder he was exhausted! His gaze traveled slowly around the corral. He brushed his dark hair out of his face and took in the other horses and the new stationmaster, Josh Wiggins. At last his deep blue eyes rested on Lexie. He went to her, holding out his hands. "Lexie!" he exclaimed. "I heard about your father. I'm so sorry!"

"Thank you," she said. Billy pressed her hand between both of his and looked into her face.

"I was out at Elkhorn Station when I heard," Billy said finally. "Is the funeral . . . am I in time?"

Lexie shook her head. "It's over now. But he wouldn't have expected any of the riders to be there," she assured him. "The mail has to go through."

While Josh Wiggins got busy rubbing down Billy's horse, Lexie and Billy went into the station. Lexie poured him some coffee and ladled out a bowl of soup. Billy was ravenous, and she decided to hold off on asking her questions until he finished eating. But just as Billy was refilling his bowl, Josh Wiggins bustled in. "Got your pony all tucked away," Josh told Billy. "Feisty little devil! Bared her teeth at me when I took off her halter!"

"She's fast, though," Billy said. "Coming over the mountain from Deer Creek we ran two miles neck and neck with an antelope!"

She couldn't ask about Callum in front of Wiggins. Callum was a wanted man. If Billy knew where he was hiding, it would be a well-kept secret.

"There's a bad stretch of trail back there, from Box Elder to Little Muddy," Billy was saying. "Washed

30

out in a big rain last week."

Lexie picked up a coil of rope that lay on the table. As Josh and Billy talked about the weather, she twirled it into a series of knots—bowline, sheepshank, clove hitch. "Let me see that!" Billy exclaimed, glancing over at her. "Where'd you learn all those?"

"Papa showed me," she said, holding up the rope for both men to admire. "It was something to do on winter nights."

"It's a good skill to have," Billy said, sliding the rope through his hands. "I wish somebody would teach me sometime."

"I'll show you," Lexie said eagerly. "It's not as hard as it looks."

"Not now," Billy said with a long, contented sigh. "My brain is tired. My body's tired. Even my hands are beat."

Suddenly, hoofbeats thundered up the trail toward the station, and the blast of a horn announced the incoming eastbound rider. Wiggins sprang for the door with a brisk "Hello!" Lexie heard the horse stamping and blowing as the rider pulled it to a halt. She and Billy listened to the voices and clatter in the yard. At last Lexie took a deep breath and asked, "When you're out on the trail, do you ever hear news about my brother?"

Billy looked down at the scarred tabletop. "You want to send him word about your father, is that it?"

"Do you know where he is?" she pressed.

Billy didn't meet her gaze. "I'll see that he gets the news," he said. "Wherever he is."

Lexie's heart raced. She fought to keep her voice steady. "You know, don't you? Where is he?"

"I don't know anything for certain," Billy protested. "You hear things along the trail, but half of it's just rumors."

"Not the other half, though," Lexie pointed out. "You hear a lot that's true."

Billy nodded reluctantly. "He can't live in the open, you know," he said, and there was a warning note in his voice. "He can't even use his own name now."

"I'm not the law!" Lexie insisted. "I'm his sister. And he's the only family I've got left."

"Somebody told me you have an aunt out east," Billy said. "I hear you'll be going to live there."

"That's what they want me to do," Lexie said. "The reverend and his wife. But I want to find Callum.

Even if they knew where Callum is, they'd never let me go to him. They think he stole that ring."

Billy snorted. "Callum never cared about money. And he loved riding with the Pony. Why would he give up his job for a silly piece of metal?"

"He wouldn't!" Lexie said fervently. "I know that, and Papa knew—and you know it too." Lexie looked at him. He truly was Callum's friend.

"Still, to people who don't know Callum, his story is pretty weak," Billy sighed. "The stationmaster at Green River swore Callum never showed up, never brought in his mochila."

"But he got a fresh horse," Lexie said. "He came back with a mochila heading east."

"And there was nothing in it," Billy said. "It was full of straw, remember?"

"Of course I remember!" Lexie exclaimed. "I was there. There was a terrible snowstorm, but Callum came in on time. The next rider was late, and while we waited, a messenger galloped in from Green River. He claimed Callum and the mail had never gotten there."

"So Callum showed his mochila?" Billy asked. "As proof?"

"Yes," Lexie said, sighing. "Only, when I took a good look at it, I knew something was wrong. Callum's mochila had no locks on it. The messenger from Green River noticed the same thing. He tore open the flaps and gave the mochila a shake."

"And straw fell out," Billy said, shaking his head. "I heard about that."

"Nothing but straw," Lexie said. "Callum was as shocked as the rest of us. He just stared at that big cloud of straw floating over the table. But the messenger told him, 'You're a liar.'" Lexie shuddered at the memory.

"I've thought and thought about it," Billy told her. "It doesn't make any sense to me. But I know Callum is innocent."

"Callum wouldn't want me to go live in New York City," Lexie stated. "I'm the only family he's got too."

Billy leaned his chin on his hand. He seemed to make up his mind. "Well, I've heard he's somewhere near Salt Lake City," he said carefully. "How about you write him a letter? I'll make sure it reaches him."

"All right. I will. Thank you, Billy," Lexie said. She really ought to get back to the parsonage. People would be looking for her, wanting to tell her how sorry they were about Papa. They weren't all like those women in the kitchen, she reminded herself. Many people in Willow Springs had been kind to her and Callum as they were growing up, and they all respected Papa. It was her duty to be with them now, just as Mrs. Harkness said.

She got to her feet. "I have to go now. How long will you be here?"

"Bring me your letter by midnight," Billy said. "I'll be heading farther west."

As Lexie stepped outside, she heard pounding hooves and saw a puff of dust disappear over the crest of the ridge. The eastbound Pony rider was off. Waving to Josh Wiggins, she mounted Cougar and set out for the parsonage.

Mrs. Harkness was waiting for her as she cantered into the yard. She began talking before Lexie's feet left the stirrups. "Where have you been? We've been looking all over for you! All of our guests wanted to see you! I told you to sit in the parlor, and instead you go off on that horse of yours like some wild In—" She stopped herself, but the unspoken word hung in the air.

"I needed some time alone," Lexie said as she tied Cougar to a fence post. She would have to rub him down later. "Here's your skirt. Thank you for letting me wear it."

Mrs. Harkness took the black funeral skirt and gave it an angry shake. "You wore it riding!" she said, appalled. "On a man's saddle!"

Lexie couldn't argue. In silence she tried to wait out the storm.

"It's disgraceful!" Mrs. Harkness said, shaking her head so that the ribbons on her bonnet quivered. "If you run off like this on the day of your father's funeral, you're capable of almost anything! This country is a dangerous influence on a young girl. Especially a girl who—"

Again Lexie felt a surge of pain and anger. She couldn't hold her tongue any longer. "Especially a girl who's half Arapaho?" she asked.

Mrs. Harkness flushed. "Don't you be saucy with me, young lady!" she snapped. "My husband and I want to do the best we can for you, for your poor father's sake."

"I know that," Lexie said, struggling to regain her composure. "I appreciate everything you've done for me. I really do." In the awkward silence Lexie cast a longing glance at Cougar. She wanted to take him into the field and give him a good rubdown.

"Come inside," Mrs. Harkness said, to Lexie's disappointment. "Mr. and Mrs. Jenkins are waiting to see you."

Lexie trailed after her into the parsonage. Will Jenkins, the carpenter, sat stiffly in the parlor beside his sharp-faced little wife. They rose and held out their hands when Lexie entered. "We're so sorry about your father," May Jenkins said. "Such a shame! He was a wonderful man!"

"He was, yes," Lexie said. "Thank you." She didn't know what else to say. For a few moments she held May Jenkins' hand awkwardly, not sure when she should let it go.

"You ought to be grateful that you have a place here with the pastor," Mrs. Jenkins went on. "An orphan girl should always show her gratitude."

"Now, May," Will Jenkins began mildly. He broke off as his wife turned on him with a deadly frown.

"This young lady has a lot of hard lessons ahead of her," Mrs. Jenkins continued. "No more of this aimless riding on every whim. She needs to learn to help indoors and stay out of mischief."

Mrs. Harkness sighed. "She'll have to learn how to behave properly in New York, but we are obliged to wait until her aunt sends a reply."

May Jenkins looked at Lexie with a stern eye. She sniffed and said, "It would be better to send her to her aunt right away. If you like, we can take her with us when we leave for St. Joseph tomorrow."

"Tomorrow!" Lexie cried, but no one seemed to hear her.

"St. Joseph? Of course, that's not far from New York City!" Mrs. Harkness exclaimed. "Perhaps it would work. If you could telegraph her aunt as soon as you get to St. Joseph . . ."

"Of course!" Mrs Jenkins said, nodding. "And when we get an answer, we'll put the girl on the train for New York."

Nothing they said seemed real. They sounded as if they were discussing a package of mail. They couldn't be planning for her to leave tomorrow!

"It would be such a relief to send her on her way," Mrs. Harkness said. "The thought of having to keep my eyes on her all winter—I just don't know how I'd manage!"

"We'll come by in the wagon at sunup," Mr. Jenkins said, glancing at his wife for her approval. "She'll have to be all ready to go."

Lexie felt as though the earth was giving way beneath her feet. "What about Cougar?" she asked desperately. "I can't leave him! Who will take care of him?"

"My husband will put him up for sale," Mrs. Harkness said. "The proceeds will go toward your traveling expenses to New York."

"For sale!" Lexie cried. "Cougar? You'd sell him to a stranger?"

"It's only a horse," Mrs. Harkness told her. "You should be thinking about more important things at your age!"

In a daze Lexie listened to them talking about trunks and boxes and the cost of a second-class ticket. She couldn't be parted from Cougar! There must be something she could do! She had to make a plan—tonight—or she'd be on her way to New York in the morning.

"You'll be better off in St. Joseph," Mrs. Jenkins told her as she and her husband rose to go. "We will be staying at the Patee House. It's a fine hotel, and you'll have to learn some decorum. But it will go some way toward preparing you for New York."

The words echoed around her like the squawks of a jay. Another set of words filled her head, blocking out everything else. *I can't go east*, she thought. *I can't go east. I have to find Callum!*

There was no time to send Callum a letter with Billy Cates, no time to wait for an answer to make its way back along the trail. She had to go herself and find Callum. Wherever he was, she would tell him herself about Papa's death. Then she could stay with him, and they would take care of each other.

Finally, Mrs. Harkness excused her to go and tend to Cougar. Lexie went into the field, determination filling her with every step.

As she unsaddled Cougar and rubbed him down, she told him, "I won't let them sell you! They won't take you away from me." Cougar leaned his head against her shoulder as if he knew how she felt.

Lexie made up her mind. She'd slip out of the parsonage when everyone was asleep and ride back to the station. She'd see Billy before he left and ask him to help her. He could tell her how to get to Salt Lake City, following the Pony Express trail through the mountains. If Callum could make the journey, she knew she could make it too. She could do it, with Cougar's help.

✶ Chapter Four ✶

After exchanging polite "good nights" with the reverend and his wife, Lexie went to her room and closed the door. A windowless closet at the back of the parsonage, it had once been used by the Harknesses' servant woman. The servant had left a year ago, and Mrs. Harkness had given the room to Lexie for the duration of her stay.

Lexie opened the pine box and spread its contents carefully on her coverlet. There a stone she had found on one of her rides with Cougar. It was embedded with quartz crystals that glittered like jewels.

There was an eagle feather that had floated down from the sky one morning and landed at her feet like a gift from the heavens. There was a chunk of limestone scored by a strange, birdlike footprint, as though some forgotten creature had left its mark long ago. Lexie counted the three silver dollars that Aunt Grace had sent her last Christmas. She needed to travel light, but those dollars might well come in handy.

At the bottom of the box, wrapped in a white linen handkerchief, lay a necklace made out of blue glass beads. Lexie unwrapped it gingerly and slid the beads through her fingers. She knew that they weren't really valuable, but she loved the way that they sparkled in the candlelight. Papa had given her the necklace one day last summer. "It was your mother's," he said simply. "Maybe you'd like to have something that belonged to her."

It was a very precious gift, and Lexie had been thrilled. For a few days she wore the necklace everywhere she went. Then Callum warned her that she might lose it on one of her wild gallops out on some mountain trail, and she put it away in her box for safekeeping. Now she studied the clasp and realized that it was well made and sturdy. She felt she could trust it after all. By the light of the candle she fastened the necklace about her neck. It lay against her skin, cool and somehow comforting.

If only she had some memento of Papa to carry with her too! He hadn't owned much beyond the basic necessities—shirts and pants, a pair of Sunday shoes, and a bentwood rocking chair, which he liked to sit on in the evenings. Suddenly, Lexie's eyes fell upon the handkerchief that had held her mother's necklace. In the bottom left corner she read the embroidered initials: R. M. M. "Robert Malcolm McDonald," she murmured. Of course! This was Papa's handkerchief. She folded it tenderly and slipped it into the pocket of her skirt. She was glad that she had added good deep pockets when she split and resewed the skirt for riding.

Lexie returned everything else to the box. It gave a thin, hollow rattle as she set it down in the corner. She would have to leave it behind, with all the treasures from her childhood. She had no more room in her life for feathers and pretty stones, she thought. Nothing mattered now but to keep Cougar and to find Callum.

From her pocket she took a pen, an ink jar, and a

folded sheet of paper that she had brought from the parlor. By the candle's flickering flame she wrote:

Dear Reverend and Mrs. Harkness,
I am very grateful for all the help you have given me. You have been most generous, and I will always remember you. However, I feel I cannot go to live with my aunt in New York, and I have made other plans. Mr. and Mrs. Jenkins should go on without me. Please do not worry about me. I will be all right. I wish you the very best of everything.
Sincerely,
Alexandra McDonald

Lexie reread the letter phrase by phrase, wondering what Mrs. Harkness and her husband would say when they found it tomorrow morning. They'd be furious, no matter what dainty words she chose. They'd probably send someone out to look for her. By that time she'd be well on her way. With Cougar's speed and a bit of luck, they'd never catch up with her.

First she had to escape from the parsonage and reach the Pony station before Billy Cates left at midnight. Should she carry the candle and take the chance that someone would glimpse the light? Or should she sneak out in the dark and risk waking the house by banging into a cupboard or a chair? She decided to take the candle. The most important thing was to leave quickly and silently.

With extreme care, inch by agonizing inch, Lexie opened the door to her room. The hinges were blessedly noiseless. She slipped into the hall in her stocking feet and pulled the door shut behind her. On tiptoe she crossed the kitchen, pausing to listen outside the closed door of the room where Mrs. and Reverend Harkness slept. To her relief, someone was snoring, as long and loud as the rumbling croak of a bullfrog. She took a deep breath and dashed past the door and across the parlor. The front door swung open at her touch, and with a racing heart, she stepped out into the clean night air.

Cougar whinnied when she entered the barn. He stretched his head over the top of the stall door, eager to greet her. "Ssh!" she whispered, crouching to pull on her shoes. "We're not safe till we get on the trail!"

Pale moonlight streamed through the barn door, and she did not need a lantern. Cougar stood quietly as she placed the saddle on his back. They never went riding at this time of night, but he didn't seem startled by the change in routine. He seemed to sense that they were embarking on a very important adventure.

Once they were on their way, cantering over the hill toward the station, Lexie found herself wondering about her own judgment. She'd always loved the map of the Pony Express trail that hung just above their fireplace, and she knew by heart the names of the stations and the distances between them. Salt Lake City was 140 miles away. Carried by a series of Pony Express riders who changed horses every ten to 15 miles, a mochila could travel from Willow Springs to Salt Lake City in one day. Through the company's carefully devised relay system, the Pony riders kept the mail moving at nine miles per hour or more for most of the way.

Lexie knew that Cougar could not possibly keep up such a pace for long. Like most of the Pony Express horses, he ran like an antelope when he was fresh and bursting with energy. But after such a burst he needed time to recover. As she followed the trail, she would have to give him plenty of time to feed and rest. It might take her two days—or even three—to cover the distance. She'd never been more than half a day's ride from Willow Springs before. Could she and Cougar make it? They would have to try.

Lexie pushed her fears aside and straightened in the saddle. It was too late to worry about things that might happen. She had made up her mind to find Callum, and that was what she was going to do.

The station was quiet when Cougar drew to a stop. A few wisps of smoke curled from the chimney, the last traces of a dying fire. A little black mare stood in the corral, stamping her forefeet impatiently. Lexie recognized her as Brimstone, a horse that had stabled at Willow Springs dozens of times since the Pony Express began. Brimstone stood ready to carry Billy Cates on the next leg of his journey, and that meant he hadn't left yet.

Lexie dismounted, loosened Cougar's saddle, and left him in the corral to wait with the mare.

Her hand was on the door handle when she heard footsteps inside the cabin. The door swung open, and Billy peered out at her.

"Did you bring the letter?" he asked in a low voice.

Lexie stared at him in bewilderment. She was so caught up in her new plan that she had forgotten about Billy's promise to take a letter to Callum. "No," she said. "I'm going to Callum myself. Tonight."

Billy stepped outside and shut the door behind him. "What are you talking about?" he demanded. "Don't

48

you know how far it is to Salt Lake City?"

"A hundred and forty miles," she said, her voice level. "I can do it. Cougar's a good horse."

"He's a fine horse," Billy said. "But you're a girl! You can't make a journey like that by yourself!"

"Why can't I?" she retorted.

"There are rattlers and cougars and grizzlies," Billy said, ticking off each hazard on his fingers. "There are horse thieves and rock slides and streams to ford. Some places the trail goes right along the rim of a cliff. If you fell, nobody'd even know to look for you."

For a moment Lexie's own fears rushed out again to taunt her. She hadn't thought about horse thieves or lying bloody and broken at the foot of a precipice. But again she refused to listen to her inner doubts. "I've met lots of rattlers," she said. "And I've ridden along ridges where there's no trail at all."

Billy tried a different tack. "I'll give you paper," he said. "Write Callum a letter, and I'll see that he gets it."

"I can't go back to the parsonage," Lexie explained. "They're going to make me leave tomorrow, for New York."

Billy looked surprised. "Tomorrow?" he repeated. "Don't they have to make arrangements first?"

"They've made them. I'm going with people from town as far as St. Joseph."

Billy shook his head sadly. "New York," he sighed. "That's so far—you might never come back."

"I'm not going!" Lexie insisted. "I told you—I'm going to Salt Lake City! I can start out with you tonight. I'll stop and rest at Pony stations along the way, and then if another rider is leaving, I'll ride alongside him. That way I'll have company, at least some of the time."

Billy was quiet, thinking. "It'd be different if you were a boy," he said at last. "A boy could make it, if he was a good rider. But a girl . . ."

"I'm as good a rider as any boy in Wyoming!" Lexie protested.

"Look," Billy said, "most of the Pony riders are fine people, but you meet a lot of rough characters on the trail too. It isn't like riding around Willow Springs, where everybody knows you. Out there—" he made a wide gesture toward the west, "there are men that'll kill you for anything. For that string of beads you're wearing."

"I can outrun them," Lexie said. "Cougar is fast."

"They've got fast horses too."

"You're not going to change my mind," Lexie said. "I've already decided."

Billy turned back to the cabin. "Then I'll wake up Josh Wiggins," he warned her. "He'll keep you here till they come from the parsonage to get you."

Lexie's heart lurched. She thought quickly. "Fine," she said, looking him hard in the face. "And you can tell Callum you handed me over against my will. You can tell him I wanted to join him, and you were the one who stopped me."

Somewhere in the distance an owl uttered a mournful cry. Billy paced to the corral fence and leaned against a post. "What am I supposed to tell him if something bad happens to you?" he groaned. "How can I say I let his little sister set out to travel a hundred and forty miles through the wilderness?"

Suddenly, an idea flashed into Lexie's head. It was as clean and cold as a knife blade and razor sharp. "Don't think of me as Callum's sister," she said. "Think of me as a boy. From now on my name is Alex."

As soon as the words were spoken, she knew what she had to do. There was no time to think. She didn't dare lose her momentum. As Billy watched, openmouthed, she dashed into the barn and emerged

51

with Papa's shears. Lifting her long, heavy hair with one hand, she opened the blades with the other.

"Don't!" Billy cried.

She couldn't stop, or she'd never gather the courage to start again. She closed the shears over the skein of hair in her hand and squeezed hard. She felt a tug and heard a sickening tearing sound. Dark spirals floated to her feet. Again she heard Billy's voice, "No, Lexie! Don't!"

✶ Chapter Five ✶

With cut after cut, Lexie's hair tumbled to the ground. At last she felt only a fringe above her ears, as ragged as a cattle-grazed field. The night wind blew cool against her unprotected neck.

Billy stared at her in shock. "You don't take 'no' for an answer," he said finally. "I can't believe you did that!"

"I did, and it's done," Lexie said. She felt giddy with excitement. There was certainly no going back now.

"Here, let me even that up a little." Billy took the shears and made a few careful snips so that her hair lay sleek and smooth all around.

"Thanks," Lexie said. "I'll put on some of Callum's clothes. Then I'll be ready to go."

"I don't know how I'm going to explain this to him," Billy muttered, but he didn't try to stop her.

In the cabin Lexie pulled a shirt and a pair of Callum's buckskin britches from a cupboard. While Josh Wiggins snored in the back room, she slipped into her brother's clothes.

From the pocket of her skirt she took her silver dollars and Papa's handkerchief and transferred them to Callum's britches. In moments she was outside again, dressed as a boy. "I'm ready when you are," she told Billy as she rebuckled Cougar's saddle girth.

Billy was sweeping up the hair that littered the yard. He put down the broom and strode toward her. "Just one thing," he said. "Boys generally don't wear beads!"

Lexie felt her face flush. She unclasped the necklace and slipped it into a pocket.

"Pleased to meet you, Alex," Billy said, holding out his hand. Grinning, he grasped her hand and gave it a vigorous shake, man to man.

"Pleased to meet you, too," Lexie answered, with a slight bow.

Billy pulled out his watch and strained to see the hands

in the moonlight. "It's time we got started," he said. "Unless I can change your mind?"

It was one of those questions that didn't deserve an answer. Lexie walked back to Cougar, ready to spring into the saddle. She paused to run a hand over the back of her head. Would she ever get used to the feel of her strange, short-cropped hair?

"Just one more thing," Billy said. "Don't walk so dainty. Take nice long steps. Like this." He strode across the yard, his arms swinging loosely at his sides.

Lexie opened her mouth to protest that she didn't walk daintily, not like the girls in town with their tight, fancy shoes. But she'd never actually watched herself walk the way that Billy watched her walking now. If she wanted to convince people that she was a boy, she'd better listen.

"Like this?" she asked. Concentrating on her feet, she walked up and down the yard. Her riding skirt had given her freedom of movement but always with yards of fabric swirling around her legs. In Callum's britches she could reach her feet far forward with each step, completely unencumbered. She practiced swinging her arms the way Billy showed her.

"That's better, Lex—I mean, Alex," Billy said at

last. "And when you stand talking, put your hand in your pocket."

"Thanks," Lexie said. She thrust her hand into her left front pocket and felt the blue bead necklace nestled at the bottom, with Papa's handkerchief for company.

"Keep it in your mind that you're a boy," Billy advised. "If you keep repeating it in your head, maybe acting like a boy will come by itself."

"Anything else I need to know?" Lexie asked.

Billy hesitated. "Well," he said, "when a fellow talks to you, don't look at him out of the sides of your eyes like a girl being shy. Look him in the face, good and forthright."

Was he saying that she didn't look forthright when she talked to him? Again Lexie bit back words of protest and tried to store the suggestion in her mind.

"Is that all?" she asked.

"The thing I worry about," said Billy, "is what will happen if someone picks a fight with you."

Lexie winced. She thought of all the times that Callum had come home with an eye black and swelling or with blood streaming from his nose. Sometimes the fight started when a boy from town called Callum a dirty Indian. At other times the

trouble seemed to break out for no reason at all.
"Boys just fight," Callum used to tell her as he wiped
away the blood. "Especially when they don't have
enough to keep them busy." With their tight
schedule, Lexie figured that the Pony riders had no
time for idle entertainment. But those rough
characters Billy warned her about had plenty of
empty hours to fill.

"I'm quick on my feet," she said hopefully. "And
Cougar can get me away from them fast. I'll manage."

"Just keep quiet and mind your own business," Billy
told her. "Don't tell anybody more than they need to
know. Keep to yourself."

"I don't want trouble," Lexie said. "I just want to get
to Salt Lake City and find Callum."

Billy touched one of the pistols hanging from his
belt. "Sometimes trouble chases you whether you want
it or not," he said, shaking his head. "That's why Pony
riders are armed."

"I know how to shoot," Lexie insisted.

"Well, you better have a gun then." Without
ceremony, Billy unclipped one of his holsters and
handed it over to her. "Don't use it unless you have to,"
he said. "Carry it wherever you go."

Lexie slid the pistol from its leather holster and turned it over in her hands. It was cold and solid and strangely heavy for its size. It brought her mingled feelings of comfort and dread. "Thanks, Billy," she said. "Thank you for everything."

Billy went over to Brimstone and picked up her reins. "Let's get started," he said. "Next station west is Horse Creek."

Lexie put a foot in the stirrup and sprang into the saddle. As she gathered up the reins, she felt Cougar quiver with excitement. With a whinny of challenge, he surged past Brimstone, keeping a full length between them as they thundered along the trail. Billy let out a whoop that Lexie could just hear over the pounding of hooves.

The Pony Express trail out of Willow Springs followed the bending course of the Sweetwater river. For the first two or three miles the trail was fairly level, and the horses kept up a vigorous gallop. Soon, however, the river plunged between rocky cliffs, and the trail climbed steeply above the water. The horses slowed to a canter and finally settled into a brisk, steady walk. "You could maybe rest up a while when you get to

Three Crossings," Billy said. Lexie had the sense that he had been mapping her journey in his mind as they rode. She knew that Three Crossings was the next home station. If all went well, she thought, she and Cougar would reach it a little after sunup.

"The next westbound rider is a nice fellow," Billy went on. "He'd be glad to have you ride with him."

"The next mail won't come through till Monday, though," Lexie protested. "I'm not going to sit around at a station waiting."

"You ought to have company as much as you can," Billy insisted. "I don't want you taking any chances."

"I don't need anyone to take care of me," Lexie tossed back. "I'm a boy, remember?"

"So you say," said Billy, mustering a laugh. "But I want to tell Callum I did my best to make you travel safe."

"Have you seen him?" Lexie asked, changing the subject. She wasn't going to wait until Monday. "What does he do in Salt Lake City?"

"I haven't seen him face-to-face," Billy admitted. "My run doesn't take me that far west. I've just heard things—you know how rumors go."

"What has he been doing—according to the rumors?" Lexie wanted any information she could get.

"Catching mustangs up in the mountains," Billy told her. "That's all I've heard."

They rode for a while in silence. The trail reached the top of the cliff and snaked along the rim. Wide and well-worn by countless Pony riders and other travelers, it gave the horses secure footing. Cougar tugged at the bit, wanting to go faster, but Lexie held him back. A long journey stretched ahead, and she didn't want to tire him right at the start.

The trail dipped toward the river once more. In some places it was so strewn with loose rocks that the horses had to pick their way, step by cautious step. As soon as the ground became clearer, they broke into a jouncing trot that gobbled the miles. At last Billy spurred Brimstone to a pounding gallop again, and Lexie couldn't resist letting Cougar join her. He hurtled forward until he was running at the black mare's side.

Suddenly, Billy swung the horn from the back of his saddle and blew three echoing blasts. "Horse Creek Station is right up there," he said, pointing. "I don't think your pony will be able to keep up when I get a fresh mount."

Lexie felt a sinking sensation in her stomach. She knew Billy was right, and for an instant she felt desolate at the thought of parting from him. "I guess we should say good-bye then," she said. "Maybe we'll meet later on, when you're riding east."

"I hope so," Billy said. "I'll try to send word to Callum, tell him you're on the way."

In the next moment the station came into view. It was a little square hut perched precariously on a steep hillside. The stationmaster, a skinny, rumpled man with a dirty beard, held a stamping palomino by the halter. The horse snorted and tried to rear as Cougar and Brimstone came to a heaving stop.

Lexie must have seen Pony riders change horses a hundred times, but the process still amazed her. Now she watched again, in awe and delight, as Billy slid to the ground and lifted the mochila from Brimstone's saddle. He flung it across the palomino's back and worked it into place so that the four pouches hung evenly, one at each corner of the saddle. Then he leaped aboard and picked up the reins. "I know this fellow," he said, patting the palomino's neck. "You're my old friend Tarnation."

Tarnation lowered his head and arched his back, kicking his rear legs into the air. "None of your tricks now," Billy said, pulling the horse's head up sharply.

"We've got mail to carry!"

"Who's your friend?" the stationmaster asked, waving a hand toward Lexie.

"Oh, this is . . . Alex Miller," Billy said. "He's on his way to meet up with some relatives."

Lexie hadn't thought about her need for a new last name, and Billy had realized that she couldn't go by McDonald. Everyone on the trail would have heard of Callum McDonald, and word of her father's death would have traveled up and down the trail by now. The name McDonald might lead to too many difficult questions.

Again Tarnation tried to buck, and again Billy Cates brought him under control. Waving to the stationmaster, he set off up the trail at a dead run.

Never happy to lag behind, Cougar left the station with a burst of speed. "Whoa there!" Lexie cried, hauling on the reins. "Settle down, boy!" Resignedly, Cougar slowed to a smooth, steady canter. Tarnation's hoofbeats faded into the distance, and at last Lexie and Cougar were alone.

Even in the moonlight the trail was easy to follow. In a few places it was marked by blazes on tree trunks, but for the most part it was a clear, well-traveled path. At times it looped away from the riverbank, but Lexie could still hear the gurgle of water off to her left. Once they crossed a meadow, loud with the rasping of crickets. Later the trail twisted through a field of rocks and boulders that seemed to stretch for miles. Cougar slowed to a walk, placing his hooves with care over the stones. When Lexie thought the rocks would never end, Cougar carried her through a narrow passage between two monstrous, overhanging boulders. On the far side she glimpsed the outline of a low building that had to be the next relay station, Devil's Gate.

In the first moment after they arrived Lexie felt a pang of disappointment. No one was waiting to greet them. Well, she reminded herself, no one knew they were on their way. Billy had already come and gone; Tarnation, unsaddled and content, was grazing at the far side of the corral. Lexie dismounted and fed Cougar a double handful of oats from his saddlebag. She led him to a lush patch of grass and gave him a hasty rubdown while he grazed. After a short rest she climbed into the saddle again and set off once more.

She missed having Billy Cates beside her. Whether they talked or rode together in silence, he was pleasant company. Yet, as the night passed, Lexie found that she also enjoyed the solitude of the empty trail. When she came to Split Rock, the next relay station, she found herself yawning and longing for sleep, but she refused to stop. The first faint signs of dawn were streaking the sky. She made a promise to herself that she and Cougar would reach Three Crossings by full daylight.

✶ Chapter Six ✶

At the top of a ridge overlooking Three Crossings Station, Lexie reined Cougar to a halt and sat still, gazing out at the sunrise. She had grown accustomed to the pale moonlight that guided her way through the night. Now the golden globe of the sun vaulted over the mountains to the east, and suddenly its brightness exploded across the whole sky. The world shimmered with the promise of a new day. Only a week ago she and Papa had watched the sunrise together as they waited for the eastbound Pony rider to arrive in Willow Springs. Now she was an orphan, heading west on a mission to find her brother.

So much had happened in only a few days' time, but the sun rose the same as always.

"Three Crossings! We did it!" she told Cougar triumphantly. "You deserve a good rest!" She clicked her tongue, and they clattered down the stony slope to the station.

The home station at Three Crossings was even smaller than the one at Willow Springs. It was a ramshackle cabin of rough logs. The roof was higher at one side and seemed to sag toward the other, as though it was ready to collapse from weariness. At the sight of it, Lexie felt her own exhaustion strike her like a blow. She had been awake for 24 hours now, and she had ridden all night with hardly a stop. She was hungry, too, but she needed sleep more than anything else.

A towheaded boy of around 13 swung open the corral gate. "I bet you're Alex Miller," he said, grinning.

It took a moment for Lexie to recognize her new name. She ran her hand over her hair, reminding herself again who she had become. "Right," she said, deepening her voice to try to sound more like a boy. "Billy Cates must have told you."

"He said we should be on the lookout," the boy explained, nodding. "Said you'd be pretty tired by the time you rode in."

"I guess I am," Lexie admitted. "My horse has had a hard ride. Can I let him rest in your stable?"

"Sure," the boy said, nodding. Lexie climbed stiffly from the saddle. Her legs felt weak and wobbly beneath her.

"Your horse is a beauty," the boy said. "Give him some oats and a couple forks of hay. Then come inside. My mother'll want to feed you."

The boy followed as Lexie led Cougar to the barn. Cougar's head drooped as she unfastened his saddle and bridle. Lexie knew how he felt. She was trembling with weariness herself.

The towheaded boy, on the other hand, was bursting with energy, and he never stopped talking. "I'm Amos Squires," he announced. "My father ran off to California last year to get rich, so now it's just me and my ma to run the station. That makes me the stationmaster, wouldn't you say?"

Lexie nodded mechanically as she rubbed Cougar's flanks with a rough horse blanket. "I want to be a Pony rider," Amos went on. "My mother thinks I'm too young. But I could pass for fourteen, and they'll take you when you're fourteen, right? I saw a notice in the post office. It said they're looking for boys fourteen to twenty-one. And it said, 'Orphans preferred.' That's because being a Pony rider is so dangerous. And I'm half an orphan, now that Pa ran off."

So tired she could barely stand upright, Lexie filled the manger with hay. When Cougar was munching contentedly, she staggered into the station, with Amos at her heels.

Amos' mother, Nell, a thin, quick-moving little woman, took one look at Lexie and pointed to the back room. "You better lie down before you fall down, young man," she said sternly. "There's a bunk in the back room."

"Oh, Ma," Amos protested. "Me and Alex were just talking."

"Leave Alex in peace for a while," she said. "He's asleep on his feet."

In the back room of the station Lexie found a set of neatly made bunk beds. She drew the ragged curtain that served as a door and flung herself down full-length. Her palms were raw from clutching Cougar's reins, and from her shoulders to her knees every muscle ached. She was so exhausted that for a while she couldn't even fall asleep.

From the other room she heard the voices of Amos

and his mother. "I bet I'm older than he is," Amos said. "And he's out on the trail by himself."

"Well, he shouldn't be," said Nell. "He doesn't look a day over twelve."

"That's what you say about half the Pony riders that come through," Amos grumbled. "They get to ride and carry the mail, and I'm stuck here doing nothing. It isn't fair."

As they talked on, Lexie's thoughts drifted. She hoped what Billy had told her was true, that Callum was capturing mustangs. Callum would love the work, and he'd be good at it too. Maybe she could help him, and they'd train horses together. Would he get the news that Papa was dead, or would she have to tell him herself? Well, anyway, she would have to find him first. Salt Lake City—it was still so far away . . .

"Alex! Alex! Are you alive?"

Lexie opened her eyes to see Amos poised over her bunk with a mischievous glint in his eye. He looked as though he was ready to pounce on her and start a playful wrestling match. Lexie drew up her knees protectively and crossed her arms over her chest. If Amos got his hands on her, he'd know in a moment that she didn't have the flat chest of a boy.

"How long did I sleep?" she asked, scrambling to her feet.

"It's already noon," Amos told her.

"Oh, no!" Lexie exclaimed. "The day's half gone."

Out in the main room Nell waited with a mug of steaming coffee. "You any relation to the Millers over by Fort Laramie?" she asked. "There was an Oren Miller that cut off part of his hand with a hatchet."

Lexie pretended to ponder. "I don't think so," she said. "I never heard of them." Billy had chosen a good name for her, she realized. There were Millers scattered all over Wyoming Territory, and she could easily be related to one or another of them.

Now that she was awake enough to notice, Lexie saw that the station here at Three Crossings made Willow Springs look like a palace. The table was nothing more than a split log balanced on an upright log at each end, and the two chairs were flat-topped stumps. The walls and ceiling were caked with soot from bygone fires. But the coffee was hot and bracing, and when Nell Squires ladled out some venison stew, Lexie dug in enthusiastically.

"Are you really only twelve?" Amos asked suddenly.

"That's what my ma thinks."

"I'm fifteen," Lexie said. It felt good to tell the truth about something.

Nell looked at her skeptically. "Small for your age," she mused, and Lexie decided telling the truth hadn't been such a good idea after all. She was too small and slender to be a boy of 15. What if Nell Squires suspected that she was a girl?

Nell was still studying her. Lexie felt she was staring right into her mind when she asked, "Where are you headed?"

Billy had warned her to "keep quiet and mind your own business." The less she said about herself, the better. But Nell Squires looked like the sort of person who insisted on answers. She would need a full, believable story.

"I was working on a ranch back there," Lexie said, waving vaguely eastward. "Mama just sent word that Papa broke his leg. They need me back home."

"Where do your people live?" Nell wanted to know.

"Out beyond Fort Bridger." Lexie waved westward in the same vague way.

"This is bad country," Nell said, shaking her head. "I saw grizzly tracks the other day."

"There's been a band of horse thieves around lately too," Amos added cheerfully. He sounded as if he couldn't wait to meet them.

"I heard," Lexie said. "A couple weeks ago they stole four Pony Express horses from the Little Sandy station and sold them back to the company!"

"How could they get away with that?" Amos demanded.

"Nobody could prove it was them," Lexie explained. "They claimed they got the horses in an honest trade. The company can't run without its ponies, so they were glad to get them back."

"Those outlaws could steal the same horses and sell them back over and over," Amos said. "What's to stop them?"

"The law, sooner or later," his mother said sternly. She turned her attention to Lexie again. "How far do you plan to ride today?"

"I want to reach Green River by tonight," Lexie said. "I can stay there and let my horse rest up."

"It'll be dark before you get there!" Nell exclaimed. "Stay with us today, and get off to an early start in the morning. Then you can go all the way in full daylight."

Lexie considered this. The Pony Express riders rode

day and night, carrying the mail with all possible speed. But she didn't have to keep up such a pace. She was in charge of her own schedule. It really might make sense to wait until she had a full day of riding in front of her, but she felt uneasy around Nell Squires, with her questions and worries. The longer she stayed here, the greater the danger that Nell would pry loose the truth. Besides, now that she had rested and eaten, she was eager to be moving again.

"If I don't reach Green River, I'll stop at one of the relay stations," she said. "Big Sandy—Big Timber—it doesn't matter."

Lexie drew one of her silver dollars from her pocket and laid it on the table. "For my food and lodging," she said.

"Gracious! That's too much!" Nell exclaimed. She handed Lexie back two two-bit coins. Lexie thanked her and edged toward the door. In minutes she and Cougar would be off and away.

But Amos wasn't ready to say good-bye. "How good are you with that pistol?" he called as she stepped outside.

Lexie touched the gun on her belt. "I guess I can handle it all right."

"Want to try some shooting?" Amos asked, following

her into the sunlight. In his hand he carried a shiny pistol of his own.

"I don't have much time," Lexie insisted. "I need to get going."

"Just a little target practice!" Amos pleaded. "I want to show you what I can do." He picked up a stone the size of a hazelnut and set it on the log fence of the corral. "Now," he said, "I'll hit that pebble from thirty paces."

"Go ahead," Lexie told him, seeing there was no way out.

"Twenty-eight . . . twenty-nine . . . thirty," Amos counted, measuring his distance. Lifting the gun, he sighted along the barrel. The blast ripped through the air. The bullet tore loose a chunk of the log where the stone had rested, sending up a cloud of splinters and shavings.

"If that stone was a horse thief, we wouldn't be hearing from him anymore," Amos said with satisfaction. "All right, Alex, it's your turn."

Lexie had done plenty of target practice with Callum and Papa. She'd hunted quail and jackrabbits to improve their meals at the station. But she didn't like the thought of testing her skill today, with Amos sizing her up and Nell studying her from the doorway.

"I don't have time," she repeated. "I can't waste any more daylight."

Amos paid no attention. He picked up another stone and set it on the fence at a spot where two logs crossed. He eyed Lexie expectantly. She had no choice. No self-respecting boy in Wyoming would walk away from such a challenge.

Lexie stepped from the fence, counting her paces as she went. At 30, she turned back and set her eyes on the stone. It was the size of an egg, a little bigger than the stone that Amos had so narrowly missed. *I've hit smaller targets than that dozens of times back in Willow Springs*, she reminded herself. There was nothing to it.

She lifted the pistol and tried to take careful aim, but her hand was shaking. "Go on," Amos said with a faintly mocking grin.

Lexie willed her hand to hold steady. Without giving herself time to think, she squeezed the trigger. The pistol roared in her ears, and the force of the explosion rocked her backward. As the smoke cleared, she looked for the stone. It was gone, and the bullet had not even chipped the logs.

Amos walked to the fence to take a closer look. "You're good," he said, and his voice was filled with admiration. He turned to his mother and added, "You don't need to worry about him. He can take care of a grizzly or anything else."

Lexie checked her gun and slid it back into its holster. She tried to look calm, but inside she was jubilant. She had been tested as a boy, and she had passed!

"Cougar!" she called, giving her quail whistle to get his attention. Cougar lifted his head and went to meet her at the fence. Amos waved a wistful good-bye as Lexie picked up the reins and trotted away up the trail.

✶ Chapter Seven ✶

Riding in the night air had been cool and bracing, but now the afternoon sun glared down with brutal strength. Lexie was glad that she had shed those hot, heavy skeins of hair back in Willow Springs. Even so, she felt as though her body was roasting like a Sunday-dinner hen. Cougar, too, felt the heat. He plodded along as if the ground dragged at his hooves with every step. The next relay station was called Ice Slough, and Lexie tried to take comfort from the name. She pictured a wintry field of white fanned by fresh mountain winds. Perhaps, by some miracle, relief lay just ahead.

But Ice Slough proved to be a disappointment. In the winter it was surely the icy expanse she had been imagining. Now, however, it was nothing but a steaming, tangled marsh. "It's the sort of place that breeds malaria fever," Papa would have said. Cougar trudged through the knee-deep muck and dirty standing water.

The tepid water in the trough at Ice Slough Station wasn't much better. It had a greenish tint, and it smelled like the water in the slough itself. Cougar didn't mind a bit. Lexie let him drink because there was no other choice. When he was finished, she dipped in her hands warily and splashed her burning face. Finally she took a deep breath and plunged her face into the trough. It was amazingly refreshing. She came up for breath and dunked her head a second time before she swung back into the saddle and set off again.

Throughout the afternoon Cougar kept up a slow but steady trot. Nell Squires had been right; they would never reach Green River by nightfall. At this pace they wouldn't get much past Big Sandy. Perhaps they could rest for an hour or two and travel on to Green River in the cool of the night.

How many times did Callum ride along this trail? Lexie wondered. What had he been thinking on that snowy night as he carried the diamond ring in his mochila? Callum swore he had delivered the mail to the stationmaster at Green River. Just as he was supposed to, he had exchanged horses and ridden back to Willow Springs with an eastbound mochila. Lexie knew he hadn't meant to deceive anyone. But something had gone terribly wrong.

As she rode along, following the trail over hills, through high valleys, and along canyon rims, Lexie turned the story over and over in her mind. Callum had delivered his mochila. The stationmaster never received it. Both of them seemed to be telling the truth, yet both stories couldn't be true. "Everyone believed the stationmaster," she said aloud. "Why should they, Cougar? Maybe he stole the ring himself and pinned the blame on Callum."

Cougar flicked his ears as though eager to catch her words. "That must be it," Lexie went on with rising excitement. "There has to be a way to prove it!"

On they went, pausing at each relay station for a short rest and then pushing west along the trail again. With a glow of satisfaction, Lexie counted off each station as they left it behind—Warm Springs, South Pass, Pacific Springs, Dry Sandy, Little Sandy. The air grew cooler as twilight approached, and Lexie was determined to press on for as long as they could.

The chatter of daytime birds gave way to the chirping of crickets. Coyotes howled from hilltop to hilltop. Lexie felt a wave of sadness. In the bright sunlight she could almost forget that Papa was gone forever. Now, as the moon rose and the evening stillness folded around her, her sense of loss crashed in on her. She longed to be back with Papa at Willow Springs, waiting for the next Pony rider to come thundering in. She had ridden away from everything she had ever known. Here she was, all alone in country where she had never ventured before, heading for a place that was nothing but a name, to find a brother who might not even be there.

Callum said that their mother's people spoke to the spirits of the dead. They heard answers in the whisper of the wind and saw signs in clouds and streams. If only she could talk to Papa! It would be such a comfort if she felt that he could hear her from wherever his spirit lived now. "Papa," she said aloud, "I'm trying to find Callum so that we can stay together. There has to be a way to clear his name. That's what I want to do—prove to everyone that Callum is innocent." She couldn't be sure that Papa had heard her, but just talking to him made her feel better.

Somewhere in the darkness a twig snapped. Something rustled in the underbrush and fell silent. Lexie gripped Cougar's reins, her ears straining. Was there a grizzly out there, stalking them in the shadows? Grizzlies were huge, but they moved with barely a sound.

Cougar turned his head to look at her. Lexie saw no sign of fear in his eyes, only curiosity, as though he wondered why she was suddenly so tense. If a grizzly was prowling around, Cougar would let her know.

The night was still and clear. The sky sparkled with stars, and the moon was almost full. Its streaming light showed Lexie the rock-scattered trail ahead. Cougar had an uncanny ability to pick his way through the rubble, even when the trail seemed to disappear. He always managed to find the path on the other side. Whenever they came to a clear stretch, he broke into an easy canter, his favorite gait. Free from the heat, he was as lively and eager as ever.

Around five miles beyond Little Sandy the trail

dipped into a high-walled canyon. Cougar's hoofbeats echoed eerily as they crossed the canyon floor. Bouncing off the close, encircling walls, the echoes gave the impression that another horse was following at their heels. Even Cougar seemed to be taken in. He twitched his ears forward and back, scooping up the sound from all directions.

Lexie reined Cougar to a stop and sat in the saddle, listening. She expected a deep silence. Instead the hoofbeats kept coming. With a lurch of fear, she knew that she and Cougar were not alone.

Horse thieves, she thought in terror. She had ridden straight into a trap. Her only hope was to escape from the canyon as quickly as she could. With a sharp kick, she sent Cougar racing toward the trail at the far side. Then, from somewhere ahead and above them, she heard the snort of another horse and a man's voice shouting, "Hold it right there!"

She was caught, trapped between two men who wanted to steal Cougar. Somehow she had to save him! In one fluid gesture she wrapped the gelding's reins around the saddle horn so that they wouldn't trail behind him. In the next instant she sprang to the ground. "Go on!" she cried. "Run!"

She gave Cougar a hard slap on the rump, and he bolted in fright. Frantically, he circled the canyon, searching for a way out. At both ends horsemen blocked his escape. In the moonlight Lexie saw a break in the canyon wall, a narrow, twisting path a few yards from the main trail. Would Cougar find it in time?

"Over there!" she cried, pointing wildly. For a moment Cougar hesitated, turning his head to watch her. Then he bounded for the path that she had discovered. Earth and pebbles rained down as he scrambled desperately toward the canyon rim.

Behind her someone shouted, and a shot rang out. The walls of the canyon swelled the gun's shot to a deafening roar. Terrified, Cougar made a last gigantic leap and disappeared. Lexie was filled both with relief and with dread as she watched him go.

A moment later one of the riders on a big bay gelding seized Lexie by the collar. She fought to pry loose his hand, but he rapped her hard across the knuckles with the butt of his gun.

The other rider, on a gray horse, pressed in on her too, and the two men herded her against the wall. As they dismounted, Lexie reached for the pistol at her belt, but one of the men grabbed her arm and twisted it behind her back. "What have we got here, Driscoll?" he asked in a taunting voice. "Skinny little fella, ain't he?"

The man named Driscoll grunted and handed him a rope. Deftly, the first man tied Lexie's hands behind her. "Now what, boss?" Driscoll demanded. "We lost the horse, and we've got this little tadpole instead."

"We'd have caught the horse if you hadn't shot your gun," the first man flared.

Driscoll didn't seem phased by his boss' anger. Without a word, he unfastened Lexie's gun and inspected it carefully. Then he clipped it to his own belt. He was the shorter of the two, she noticed, thickset, with big, stubby hands. His companion was taller but stoop-shouldered and bowlegged, as though he'd spent years in the saddle. "Listen, Pike," Driscoll said, "that buckskin horse of his can't be far. I'll go look for it."

"You'll do what I tell you," Pike said, his voice as heavy and cold as an ax blade. "We'll keep moving. Somebody might have heard that shot of yours."

Pike fished in his pocket and drew out a dirty bandanna, which he bound across Lexie's eyes. Instinctively, she tried to lift her hands to tear away the blindfold, but the rope bit into her wrists and seemed to grow tighter than ever.

I'm trapped, Lexie thought in despair. No one but Billy Cates knew her plans, and it might be days before he learned that she had never reached Salt Lake City. Maybe Billy would search for her, but by then it would be too late.

Once Lexie had seen a rabbit go still with terror. It didn't even move when she bent down and picked it up. She'd felt its racing heart beneath her fingers and known that she had the power to kill it with her bare hands. It had given up hope and accepted that it was going to die. Even when she set it down in the grass again, it sat quivering for a long moment before it suddenly awoke and darted to safety. Now, as the men hoisted her onto the back of one of the horses, Lexie felt like a terrified rabbit herself. She was their captive, stunned into submission.

✶ Chapter Eight ✶

The men forced her up onto one of their horses. It felt bigger than Cougar, and Lexie guessed it must be the bay. It walked with a jarring, unsteady gait, as though it was moving over rough ground.

Lexie's journey flashed through her mind. She had slipped away from the parsonage, disguised herself as a boy, and ridden most of the way from Willow Springs to Little Sandy alone. She had made up her mind to find Callum, and nothing had stopped her yet. *I haven't come this far to give up now,* she told herself fiercely. *I am no witless rabbit!* Somehow, in some way she could not yet imagine, she would manage to survive.

Lexie knew that if she concentrated on her journey, maybe she could figure out where they were taking her. She caught the fragrance of pine on the night air and heard the soft thud of hoofbeats cushioned by a carpet of fallen needles. The horses splashed across a bubbling creek and turned sharply to the left. For a while they traveled over even ground, with the sound of the water always on their left side. Once the noise of tumbling water intensified for a few minutes, as though they were passing a waterfall. Then they turned away from the creek and began another steep ascent.

Every detail might help later on, Lexie thought. They had bound her hands and covered her eyes, but they couldn't tie up her mind. She still had a choice to make. If she gave up hope, she would be as helpless as that trembling rabbit that she had held in her hands. If she was determined to survive, she might find a way to escape.

Suddenly, the horse stopped. "Get down," Pike told her. "From here we walk."

Unable to use her hands, Lexie half climbed, half fell from the horse's back. Tall, thick grass softened her landing, and she realized that they must be in a field. She listened as Pike and Driscoll moved around her, their boots swishing through the grass as they walked. They must be staking out the horses in a place with ample grazing.

At last Driscoll clapped a hand onto Lexie's shoulder and dragged her to her feet. With his hand clenched around her upper arm, he propelled her forward. She stumbled as a fallen branch snagged her ankles, but Driscoll didn't pause. Lexie tried to kick free of the branch and fell headlong to the ground.

"What are you doing?" Pike snapped. "Keep him moving! We don't have all night!"

Driscoll muttered indignantly as he dragged her to her feet again. He gripped her arm more tightly than ever and grumbled under his breath as he hustled her along.

They started down a steep, stony slope, and Lexie stumbled again. "I can't keep dragging him like this!" Driscoll exploded. "I'm taking off the bindings whether you like it or not!"

"Suit yourself," Pike said curtly.

"Try any funny business, and you'll be sorry," Driscoll warned her with a scowl, tugging loose the ropes that bound her hands. Relieved to have movement in her arms again, she quickly reached up and pulled down her blindfold. She saw that they were in a narrow passageway between a pair of immense granite boulders. Just ahead, the passage narrowed even further, until the boulders came together, forming the entrance to a tunnel.

Pike struck a match and put a flame to the end of a stout stick. Holding it up as a torch, he led the way, crouching low beneath the overhang. Driscoll jerked Lexie's arm downward, letting her know that she should crouch, too. With a shudder, she saw that she would have to follow them into their lair. The entrance to the cave looked like a toothless mouth, waiting to gulp her down into the depths of the earth.

Driscoll shoved her ahead of him. "What're you waiting for?" he demanded. "Go on!"

On hands and knees, Lexie crawled into the tunnel. The air grew suddenly cooler. It had a stale, murky smell that reminded her of stagnant water. The stone floor felt damp and gritty beneath her hands as she scrambled deeper, following the flickering light from Pike's torch.

Within a short time, perhaps only half a minute, the tunnel widened, and the ceiling rose enough to let them stand upright. They were in a large room, roughly oval in shape. Pike took a lantern from behind a jutting rock, and the room blazed into life.

This was plainly a hideout that the outlaws used regularly. It was filled with evidence of their comings and goings—a heap of sacks, a bundle of clothes, a collection of bottles. A spot on one side seemed to serve as their garbage dump; it was piled with broken bottles and the refuse of former meals. A smell of decay mingled with the general dampness.

Lexie didn't have long to think about her surroundings. Pike stepped toward her, shining the lantern in her face, as Driscoll roughly bound her hands again behind her back. "So," he said, "you lost your horse, and you lost your mail. What are Misters Russell, Majors, and Waddell going to say about that?"

In the frantic chase back in the canyon Pike and Driscoll must not have gotten a close look at Cougar's saddle. They believed he was carrying a mochila. Lexie's thoughts raced as Pike studied her face in the lantern light. Like Cougar circling the canyon, she sought wildly for a plan that would help her escape. Pike and Driscoll believed she was a Pony Express rider. Should she try to play the part?

Maybe she could offer to lead them to information about a valuable package and at the right moment make a break for freedom.

"What're they gonna say?" Pike went on. "What'll they say when they find out their dear, sweet Pony boy lost the mail?"

The way that Pike sneered when he said "dear, sweet Pony boy" sent a chill down Lexie's spine. In an instant she understood that he despised the Pony riders for the very traits that other people admired in them: their honesty, their clean living, their determination to get the mail through on time. If he thought she was with the Pony Express, she had no hope for mercy.

"Answer me!" Pike said sharply. "Haven't you got a tongue in your head?"

"I'm not one of those Pony riders!" Lexie exclaimed, pumping her voice full of outrage. "You wouldn't catch me taking that oath that those poor fellows have to take!"

Lexie thought that maybe these men specialized in preying upon Pony Express riders. Perhaps they were the thieves who stole Pony Express horses and sold them back to the company.

Driscoll hovered at the edge of the pool of lantern light. "Then what was you doing, riding through the canyon when decent people are in bed?"

"I'm trying to join up with my brother," Lexie said. "He got in some trouble and had to clear out of town in a hurry."

"Oh?" asked Driscoll with interest. "What sort of trouble?"

"People said he stole something," Lexie said. "A lady's ring."

"Pretty little stones," Pike said, nodding. "They can be worth a lot of money."

"If you can sell them without getting caught," Driscoll said, half under his breath.

Pike glared at him. "Would you stop whining about it? We'll sell it when we can."

With a shock, Lexie made the connection. Suppose—was it possible?—Pike and Driscoll did have something to do with the disappearance of Callum's mochila six months ago!

Somehow, against the turmoil that erupted in her mind, Lexie managed to hold herself very still. Not a quiver betrayed her excitement. Pike and Driscoll had stolen one of those "pretty little stones"! And they still had it in their possession! Was it the ring that Callum had delivered to Green River?

"Where are you from, boy?" Pike asked. "What do they call you?"

"I'm Alex Miller," Lexie said and added, "from Fort Laramie." It was the first town that popped into her head.

"That brother of yours ran pretty far from home," Pike said, watching her narrowly. *I should have mentioned some town closer by*, Lexie thought. Maybe they'd have been more likely to believe her story. It was too late; she couldn't change her tale now. Instead she fell back on Billy Cates' advice. She simply shrugged and said nothing.

"What did we keep him for?" Driscoll hurled into the silence. "Did you think the Pony would pay a ransom for him?"

"Never mind what I think!" Pike shot back. "When you need to know, I'll tell you."

Pike will only keep me alive if he thinks I can be of use to him, Lexie thought. If he believed she came from a family of thieves, he might want her to join in one of their schemes. She would do her best to strengthen that belief. But suppose the outlaws realized she was a girl? They might be outraged that she had tricked them. A girl would be useless, nothing but trouble—someone to

93

get rid of as soon as possible.

Driscoll muttered and stalked into the shadows. A moment later Lexie heard the clatter of a bottle and the pop of a cork. "Bring it here," Pike ordered. Sullenly, Driscoll returned and passed the bottle to Pike, who took a long swig.

Lexie's arms ached. She tried to ease herself into a more bearable position, but the rope around her wrists gave her almost no leeway. Each time she moved it bit hard into her flesh, and she had to suppress a cry of pain.

For the moment the men seemed to have forgotten her. Grimly silent, they passed the whiskey back and forth. If only she could loosen the rope! Lexie tried to pry at the knot with her fingertips. She knew from all her practicing with Papa that the best way to untie a jammed knot was to work at it from different angles and see if anything shifted. Her hands were almost numb from being tied for so long, and the task seemed hopeless at first. Then, to her amazement, she felt something yield. Her arms were still bound, but the rope was now a little bit looser. She could have wept with relief, but again she forced herself to remain still, to reveal nothing.

Lexie watched her captors closely. With every passing moment, the tension seemed to mount between them.

When Pike spoke at last, his words flew like arrows from a taut bow. "We're gonna do Green River again."

"You're crazy!" Driscoll burst out. "It'll cost us our necks!"

"It worked before," Pike retorted.

"And a lot of good it did us!" Driscoll exclaimed.

"I didn't ask for your opinion," Pike flashed. "If you hadn't gone expressing your opinion with your pistol tonight, we'd have caught that little buckskin."

"He ain't lost," said Driscoll. "We just ain't found him yet."

Lexie was grateful that Cougar had gotten away from these men. *How many other horses would have been smart enough to find that half-hidden path?* she thought with a glow of pride. *How many others would be agile enough to climb that path without slipping? But where is Cougar now? Will I ever see him again?*

Again they lapsed into silence. After a while Driscoll stretched out on a dirty blanket and began to snore. Pike sat alone, brooding in the gleam of the lantern. He rose and paced back and forth. Lexie leaned back against the rough stone wall and went on quietly picking at the knot. She could hardly reach it at first. Then, as she felt it yield again ever so slightly, she discovered that she could turn her hands within the rope's tight grasp. Her fingers throbbed as the blood rushed back. She endured the pain, knowing it meant that her hands were coming back to life.

Pike nudged Driscoll with the toe of his boot. "I'm gonna look for that horse," he said. "Keep an eye on the boy."

Driscoll sat up and rubbed his eyes. "You ain't gonna find him till morning," he grumbled.

Pike repeated, "I'm going out." He hunched down and crawled into the tunnel. Lexie heard the fading scrape of his boots over stone, and then he was gone.

"So," Driscoll said when they were alone, "I'm supposed to keep an eye on you. That's what the boss says."

Lexie held her breath. What would he do if he checked the rope? He hadn't wanted to bring her along in the first place, and he had already shown that he was impulsive with the trigger.

Driscoll settled himself on the blanket again. He propped himself on an elbow to look at her. "You ain't much of a talker," he remarked.

"Guess not," Lexie agreed. Maybe he would fall asleep again. Then she could work on the rope some more.

"You know what I think?" Driscoll asked. "I think the boss has a plan for you."

Lexie shrugged. The less she said, the more Driscoll went on talking.

"I've got an idea what that plan is too," he declared. "He wants you to join in with us. What do you think of that?"

"Why would he want me?" Lexie asked.

"Who's gonna suspect a little runt like you?" Driscoll asked. "You could walk right past a sheriff, and he'd never blink an eye. That's what old Pike is thinking."

"How long have you been working for him?" Lexie ventured.

"I don't work *for* him!" Driscoll said vehemently. "That ain't the way it is."

Lexie fell silent again, hoping he would say more.

"He thinks he's got all the brains," Driscoll said after a while, picking up where he had left off. "He comes up with a plan, and I'm supposed to follow it." Driscoll took another long swig from the whiskey bottle, draining the last drop. Lexie heard the shatter of glass as he tossed the bottle onto the trash heap. "Pike ain't my boss," Driscoll growled. "He ought to listen to me once in a while." His gaze wandered around the cave, and he seemed to be talking to himself. Lexie watched him, alert to his every movement. "That Green River trick, it *was* clever. The Pony rider never guessed."

Driscoll lapsed into a long, morose silence. Lexie waited for him to say more, but he seemed lost in his own thoughts. "The Pony rider never guessed," she prodded.

"No," Driscoll said, "He put his pouch right in the stationmaster's hands and never suspected that he was Andrew Pike, a wanted man."

"Why?" Lexie asked, her heart pounding. "How did you get him to do it?"

"One hut looks like another," Driscoll said smugly. "Only took us half a day to build our own station."

Suddenly, it all made sense. Pike and Driscoll had set a trap for Callum, and he had ridden straight into it, unsuspecting. He had found a false station on that stormy night and had believed that he was passing his mochila to the stationmaster at Green River. If only she could shout her discovery from the mountaintops! But unless she got out of this cave, the world would never know the truth.

"Pike is so smart," Driscoll went on. "But what do you do with a diamond ring in Wyoming Territory? 'We got to be careful,' he says. 'Can't go talking it around,' he says, 'or the wrong people might get wind of it.' Six months, and we're still living like rats! With a ring worth a thousand dollars!"

Driscoll's glance flickered toward the far wall and rested on a low ledge of rock. In a fraction of a second it veered away again, but Lexie had seen it. As clear as his words, the glance had told her where the ring was hidden.

Driscoll went to the tunnel and peered out. Apparently seeing nothing, he uncorked another whiskey bottle and cradled it moodily. After a few swigs he peered down the tunnel again. "Looking for a horse!" he grumbled. "I better look for *him*!"

Driscoll patted the pistols on his belt, as though assuring himself that they were still there. He fumbled with one of the sacks that lay on the floor and pulled out a length of rope. With a lurch of dismay, Lexie realized that he hadn't forgotten about her after all. "You're staying here," he told her, twisting the rope around her ankles and tying another tight knot. As Lexie held her breath, he tested the rope on her arms with a light tug. The rope held. If he had taken the time, he would have noticed that she had worked on the knot. But she could smell the whiskey on his

99

breath; he wasn't clearheaded enough to notice.

Suddenly, Driscoll pulled out one of his pistols and pointed it at Lexie's head. "It's my turn to give the orders now!" he told her with a sneer. "Don't move!"

Lexie felt a wave of numbness sweep from her head to her toes. She couldn't have moved even if she had tried. She sat frozen, knowing that every heartbeat might be her last. She would never find Callum or clear his name, never see Cougar again.

"Good," Driscoll said with satisfaction. "Now you know who's boss around here. Just don't forget it." He slipped the pistol back into his holster, crawled into the tunnel, and disappeared.

✳ Chapter Nine ✳

Lexie was alone, and for the time being, she was safe. She had no way of knowing how long Pike and Driscoll would stay away. They might be back at any moment, or they could be gone for hours. She would be done for if they caught her trying to escape. But if she did nothing, if she threw aside this opportunity, she might be done for all the same.

Even as she pondered, her fingers pried at the knot again. She acted from pure instinct, the way a wild horse fights to escape when it is trapped behind a fence. She had to act quickly. She had no time to lose!

The knot would not yield any further. Lexie flexed her wrists, trying to slide a hand loose, but the rope still held her fast. Vigorously, she rubbed it against a rough spur of rock. After several minutes she could feel that she had hardly made any progress. There had to be a better way.

With a moment's thought, Lexie realized, *The trash heap.* It was covered with shards of broken glass from Driscoll's whiskey bottle. Lexie hitched herself along the floor until she could get a better look. Holding her breath against the stink of decay, she maneuvered to a position that allowed her to reach a large, jagged piece of glass. At first it eluded her clumsy fingers. When she finally got a firm hold of it, it sliced into her thumb, and she felt a warm trickle of blood. After three tries she managed to wedge the glass into a crack on the cave floor. As carefully as she could, she slid the rope back and forth against it, using the glass like the blade of a saw.

The rope parted so abruptly that Lexie lost her balance. As she toppled backward, the glass slashed into her arm. A knife of pain shot along her arm, and a line of crimson crept over her skin. An even greater pain tore at her as she flexed her arms. She lifted them up and down, bent them at the elbows, opened and closed her hands, and wiggled her fingers. *The pain doesn't matter*, she thought. *I'm free!*

As soon as her hands could obey her, she unbound her ankles and scrambled to the ledge where Driscoll's glance had strayed when he had mentioned the ring. Beyond the ledge she saw a shallow recess, a natural niche six inches deep. Nestled at the back, Lexie found a small, square package. The wrapping had been torn open, but she could still read the address: 46 Lombard Street, San Francisco, California.

Within the paper wrapping was something swathed in cotton batting. Ignoring the blood on her trembling hand, Lexie drew it into the open. It was a round silver box, with a butterfly engraved on the lid. Inside, resting softly on a puff of cotton, a diamond ring sparkled in the lantern light. Lexie caught her breath in astonishment. Never in her life had she seen anything so beautiful. A thousand slivers of colored light danced before her, turning that bleak underground chamber into a fairyland.

Tearing away her eyes, Lexie noticed a narrow opening in the cave wall to the right of where she stood. It was around waist height and seemed to be the entrance to another tunnel. A spider had spun a web across the opening. It was speckled with fallen sand and the dried bodies of tiny insects and looked as though it had been there, undisturbed, for a long time.

From somewhere behind her came the sound of heavy feet on stone. Someone had entered the main tunnel. Lexie hurtled back to the place against the wall where the men had left her, snatching up the discarded ropes as she ran. Suddenly, she realized that she was still clutching the ring in its silver box. She had no time to return it to its niche in the wall. Instead she shoved it into the trash heap, concealing it as well as she could beneath some moldering animal bones.

The steps drew closer. Lexie looped one rope around her ankles. She twisted her arms behind her back and draped the broken rope around her wrists. At a quick glance, it might look as though she hadn't moved.

It was Pike who emerged from the tunnel, his hair disheveled, his clothes rumpled, and his face a barely controlled snarl. Lexie waited for Driscoll to follow him, but Pike was alone.

Pike surveyed the room. His gaze passed over Lexie, scarcely taking her in. "Where's Driscoll?" he demanded.

Pike's voice rang with suspicion. He had told Driscoll to keep an eye on her, and Driscoll had disobeyed him.

Suddenly, an idea leaped into Lexie's mind. It was clear that Pike and Driscoll disliked and distrusted one another. She could use the tension between them to her own advantage. Maybe she could buy the time she desperately needed.

"He went out," she said. "A little while after you left."

"Out?" Pike repeated. "Where did he go?"

Lexie hesitated, as though she was weighing her answer. "He'd been drinking a lot," she said slowly. "He said something about going to sell a ring."

Pike lunged for the niche where the ring had lain hidden. He pulled out the torn wrapping and let it flutter to the floor. "While I was wasting my time chasing that horse!" he muttered. "The drunken idiot! I'll—" He broke off, staring at something on the floor. "Blood!" he exclaimed. "What happened here?"

"He cut himself," Lexie said, fighting to keep her voice calm. "He broke a bottle and cut his hand." Pike could trace the spots of blood along the floor, straight to the wall where she leaned. He would know that she was lying.

But he was too incensed to think. He accepted her story as though he had expected to hear it all along. "I'll kill him!" he spat as he stomped out of the cave. "He's a dead man!" His words echoed back to her as he scrambled away down the tunnel.

Lexie listened until the scraping of Pike's boots faded into silence. Carefully, she got to her feet, the ropes slithering to the ground. For a moment she pondered her choices. If she left by the main tunnel, she would know roughly where she would emerge, but she ran the risk of meeting Pike or Driscoll face-to-face. If she crawled into the tunnel that she had discovered by the niche, she had no idea where she would come out or how far she would have to go before she found an exit. She was sure that the tunnel hadn't been explored by the outlaws. The spiderweb was proof that no one had passed that way recently, and besides, the entrance was too small for the broad shoulders of grown men. If they came back and found her missing, they would not be able to pursue her.

Gritting her teeth, Lexie dug into the trash heap and fished out the silver box. She folded it into its cotton batting, tucked it back into the torn wrapping with the San Francisco address, and slipped the package into her pocket. Pike's discarded torch lay on the floor, and Lexie lit it again from the lantern.

If only she had a gun! The bandits must have a supply of weapons somewhere. It only took a moment to locate a shelf of well–used and rusted pistols. She had no choice but to grab the most reliable-looking one, and holding the torch before her, she brushed the spiderweb to dust and wiggled into the unknown tunnel.

For the first few feet the passage was so narrow that Lexie was afraid she might get stuck. To her relief, it soon grew wider and higher, and she was able to scramble along on her hands and knees. When the tunnel forked, she chose the branch that sloped upward. She longed to see the first rays of morning light, but every time she rounded a bend her torch flame probed unending blackness.

As she moved forward, Lexie lost all sense of time. The passage twisted on and on, and she felt as though she would follow it into eternity. It narrowed and widened, dipped and rose, and curled back upon itself like the shell of a snail.

Then, to Lexie's horror, the tunnel came to a dead end. The torch showed her only a blank wall of rock ahead. *I made the wrong choice at the fork*, she realized. She would have to wind her way back and follow the other branch.

In despair Lexie cast her torch beam up and down.

The wall stood solid and indifferent, offering no hope. Then, from a spot level with her head, she spied a pinprick of light. It was clean and golden—the natural light of the sun!

The light tumbled in through a hole in the cave wall, perhaps five feet above the floor. Lexie probed it with her hands and found that the edges of the hole were packed with rubble. With eager fingers, Lexie sent earth and broken stones showering down around her feet. In minutes the hole was wide enough for her head and shoulders. At last, ignoring the pain in her arm, she hauled herself through and dragged herself onto a carpet of grass. She lay there, panting, and above her stretched a vast dome of blue, open sky.

* Chapter Ten *

Lexie crouched behind a clump of bushes and peered warily around her. It was glorious to breathe in the open air, to gaze up at the endless sky, to hear the chorus of a morning's birdsong! A few feet away a creek bubbled playfully. She wondered if it was the creek that the outlaws had followed last night when they took her to the cave.

Where is the Pony Express trail? she wondered. The trails tended to follow streams and rivers. Perhaps she could find it if she traced her way along the creek.

As she walked, Lexie wondered how long it would

take for Pike to realize that Driscoll hadn't stolen the ring after all. The outlaws would rush back to the cave to investigate, and when they saw that she had escaped, they would set out together to find her. They'd assume she had taken the main tunnel, of course—the same one they used themselves. Maybe that would throw them off her trail for a while and buy her a bit more time.

The gash on Lexie's arm burned and throbbed. Her thumb ached too, a dull, steady accompaniment to every move she made. She could no longer push the pain aside. She inspected her arm in the daylight and gasped in horror. From elbow to wrist it was caked with dried blood. Her thumb was swollen and stiff, and when she bent it, bright red drops squirted out from the half-crusted wound. Her blood splattered the grass beside her. Hastily, Lexie kicked leaves over the spots. No use proclaiming to any passerby that she had been there!

What if I left a trail of blood in the cave? Lexie wondered in dismay. The telltale drops would lead straight to the tunnel by the niche, and Pike and Driscoll would know that she had not left the way she had entered. They couldn't follow her down that tunnel; it was much too narrow for either of them. But they would surely know where it emerged, and they would know exactly where to look for her.

Lexie slipped her hand into her pocket and felt the package containing the diamond ring. Driscoll had told her that this ring was worth a thousand dollars. Lexie couldn't even imagine so much money. *How can a glittering pebble on a circlet of gold be worth so much?* she thought. Such a fortune could buy the best land in the territory and the finest cattle and horses that Wyoming had ever seen. The outlaws would stop at nothing to get the precious ring back.

It isn't safe for me to stay here, Lexie decided. She needed to get away from the cave as quickly as she could. With the morning sun at her back, she began to walk westward, keeping to the fringe of trees along the bank of the creek.

Where was Cougar? Had he stayed nearby or galloped into the mountains? At least Pike hadn't found him last night. She'd rather lose Cougar forever than see him in the hands of Pike and Driscoll!

Was there a chance that Cougar was close enough to hear her if she called to him? If he heard her call, would he come to her?

Lexie stopped and scanned the horizon, searching for a moving dot that could be a riderless horse. If she found Cougar, he would help her find the trail. On Cougar's back she could put a safe distance between herself and the outlaws. His speed might mean the difference between life and death!

Lexie squatted on the ground, screened from view by the bushes and underbrush. She didn't want to risk being seen by the outlaws. She tilted back her head and sent the quail's whistle tumbling among the birdcalls around her. *Ka-HOO! Ka-HOO!* she whistled.

For an instant the air went still, as if the real birds had all been taken by surprise. Lexie strained to catch the distant thudding of hoofbeats. She heard only the rise of the birds' chorus once more.

Again Lexie gave the quail call, longer this time— and louder. The birds accepted her now and went on with their chatter and trills as if she wasn't there. Again Lexie waited, her heart pounding. *Oh, Cougar!* she thought. *Please come to me! I need you!*

But there was no response. Peering over the bushes, Lexie saw nothing but desolate, craggy peaks. She rose to her feet. Shoulders thrown back, head held high, she sent forth the quail call one last time. Its echo floated back from a boulder up ahead, a hollow remnant of her hopeful, yearning whistle.

From somewhere in the distance Lexie heard a faint rumble. It might be the threat of a coming storm. It might be a trick of her imagination. But it grew stronger and closer, and suddenly she heard a ringing neigh. She would know that sound anywhere. It was Cougar's call to her, his answer. *I'm coming!* he was calling.

She could see him now, a growing dot racing toward her from the hillside above. Neck outstretched, mane and tail streaming, Cougar came toward her at a full gallop. He didn't slow down, even when the thunder of his hoofbeats filled the air and he was only ten yards away. She almost thought he would knock her off her feet and go on running. Just in time, he swerved, racing around her in a big, joyful circle. At last, flanks heaving and foam flecking his buckskin coat, he came to a stop at her side.

"Oh, Cougar!" Lexie cried, flinging her arms around his neck. "You're the most wonderful horse in the world!"

The saddle was still on his back, though the girth had worked loose. The reins had unwound from the horn and hung from his halter in knotted loops.

Swiftly, she fixed the tangles. Her thumb protested, and her arm throbbed as she worked. Still, she reminded herself, this was a lot easier than loosening the knots that had bound her arms behind her back!

From somewhere in the distance came another low rumble. Lexie glanced at the sky. Half of it was still a radiant blue, but a bank of heavy dark clouds had moved in from the north. She heard another rumble. *Thunder*, Lexie thought. *There's going to be a rainstorm!*

Lexie would have liked to give Cougar a good rubdown after his run, but there wasn't time. If they found the trail, maybe they could reach Big Sandy before the storm struck. Lexie sprang into the saddle and turned Cougar westward. Behind her the rumble grew louder. It was a low, steady pounding. *Not thunder*, she thought with a jolt of terror. *Hoofbeats!*

Twisting in the saddle to look behind her, Lexie saw a pair of moving dots. They were coming! Pike and Driscoll were chasing her, drawing closer with each passing moment. Cougar had led the outlaws right to her.

"Giddyap, Cougar!" Lexie cried, digging her heels into his flanks. Cougar burst into a run, but his speed was hampered by the tangled underbrush and twisted piñon pines. Then Cougar veered abruptly to the right and brought her to a thin strip of cleared land. He had found the trail toward Big Sandy.

"Thank you, thank you, thank you!" Lexie breathed as he gathered speed. "I knew you could do it!"

Behind her the hoofbeats pounded closer. The dots had grown into two tiny figures, mounted men hurtling toward her in a cloud of dust. Lexie gave Cougar another fierce kick with her heels. His hooves hardly seemed to touch the ground as he surged ahead. She clung to his back, the thudding of his hooves exploding in her ears. Again she glanced behind her. The outlaws were still in wild pursuit, but Cougar was well ahead of them now. A shot rang out, too far away to put her in danger. *That must be Driscoll*, she thought. *Trigger-happy again.*

Just as she began to think that she would outrun her pursuers, another horse detached itself from the trees up ahead. A third rider was galloping toward her at top speed! It hadn't occurred to her that there might be a third outlaw. Now all three riders were working together. They would close in on her, and she would be trapped once again!

Maybe she could escape into the trees. It was her only hope. Lexie hauled on the reins, steering Cougar to the left. To leave the trail violated his training and his instincts, especially when he had been invited to run with all the speed at his command. The eastbound rider was almost on them when Cougar finally swerved and bounded off the path. In that fleeting moment Lexie saw the rider's face. Their eyes met, and she laughed aloud with joy. It was Billy Cates!

"Lexie?" he asked, amazed. "Alex?"

"Billy!" she cried. "Watch out! Horse thieves! Headed this way!"

Billy steered his horse off the trail and reversed direction to ride beside Lexie. A searing flash of lightning illuminated his face, which was filled with concern and determination. "Are they after Cougar?" he asked.

There was a shattering crack of thunder. "Yes," Lexie said as it died away. "But that's not all. I've got the ring."

"The ring that Callum—"

"Yes! That's why they're after me! They—"

The agonized scream of a horse slashed across Lexie's words. She felt a shiver of fright run through Cougar's body, and he drove himself to even greater speed. Billy let Cougar surge past him. He slowed his horse as he tried to get a better look behind them.

"Looks like one of them is down!" he called to Lexie. "One of their horses has fallen!"

Lexie pulled on the reins and slowed Cougar to a fast canter. Her gaze followed where Billy was pointing, and she saw the tumbled form of a horse, its legs thrashing in helpless pain. The thickset figure of the rider, Driscoll, broke away and vanished into the trees. But the other rider, Pike, didn't slow down. One hand held the reins, and the other brandished a pistol. Cougar had been riding hard; what if he couldn't keep going?

Suddenly, Lexie had an idea. "I don't think he saw you before you got off the trail—you were around a curve," Lexie said. "He probably still thinks I'm by myself. Your horse is fresher than Cougar. If you keep riding, he'll think you're me. You'll maintain the distance."

"Where are you going to go?" Billy asked, confused.

"There's only one of them now," Lexie said in a rush. "If we can disarm him, then there's nothing he can do. We've got to get his gun away from him." Lexie indicated to the trees. "I'm going to hide in the trees. When he passes me, I'll try to shoot the gun out of his hand. If it doesn't work, you can outrun him to Big Sandy."

Lexie didn't give Billy the chance to argue. She pulled up on the reins and urged Cougar into the trees. She glanced over her shoulder to see Billy gaining some distance on Pike.

Lexie willed Cougar to obey her, and flanks heaving, he turned to face the trail. She listened carefully. Lexie could tell by the nearing hoofbeats that it would only be a few moments until Pike passed her, and she would have to shoot at the moment that he was in front of her. There would be only one chance to shoot the gun from his hand.

Lexie took a deep, calming breath. She held the rusty pistol in her hands and hoped it would fire. As the hoofbeats pounded closer, she thought of her father's encouraging smile. *I can do this*, she said to herself. *I can do this.*

Before she realized that she had pulled the trigger, a shot rang out. Pike was in front of her, reeling back in the saddle, and for an instant, Lexie thought he had been hit. Then she saw Pike's pistol spin into the air and crash against the trunk of a tree. She had done it!

Lexie kept Pike in the sights of her gun and yelled at him to stop. At first she thought he was going to try to run for it, but he pulled up on the reins. He was caught.

Soon Billy pulled up at her side, his pistol trained on Pike as well. "That must have been an amazing shot," he said to Lexie with admiration.

Lexie's face wore a smile of triumph, but she didn't take her eyes or her gun off of Pike, who now sat hunched in the saddle, defeated.

"We're taking you to Big Sandy," Billy announced. "The law will take care of you."

Now that she had an opportunity to study him, Pike looked smaller than Lexie remembered. When he saw her watching him, his face twisted with rage. "You dirty, thieving little—" Another crash of thunder drowned his words, and suddenly the clouds ripped open. The rain gushed down in pummeling streams.

"Come on!" Billy exclaimed. "Let's get moving!" Billy kept his gun pointed at Pike's head as they rode the last two miles to Big Sandy Station. The storm roared around them, but Lexie felt like singing for joy. She had the ring, they had captured Pike, and Callum's name was going to be cleared forever. *Oh, Papa,* she thought, *soon the whole world is going to know that Callum was innocent all along!*

✶ Chapter Eleven ✶

Jack Corley, the stationmaster at Big Sandy, was a large, slow-moving man with a scraggly gray beard. His mind seemed to move with the same careful deliberation as his body. It took him some time to grasp the story that Billy and Lexie told him as they stood dripping in the station, Billy's gun still trained on Pike. "He's been stealing horses?" Corley repeated, shaking his head. "You say he stole a mochila?"

"With a ring in it," Lexie said again. "Look."

From her pocket she drew the little silver box in its tattered wrapping. Carefully, she lifted the delicate lid to reveal the ring, winking up from its cotton cushion. Pike let out an anguished groan, but no one paid any attention to him.

"That must be the ring that was stolen!" Jack exclaimed. "A Pony rider made off with it around six months ago."

"It *wasn't* a Pony rider," Billy insisted. "It was the two robbers who captured Alex last night. Pike here is one of them."

Jack Corley still seemed perplexed, even with Pike glowering from the corner. "But that boy lied," he said stolidly. "He said he brought his mochila to Green River that night."

"The outlaws tricked him," Lexie explained, struggling for patience. "They built a lean-to and made it look like the station. One of them pretended to be the stationmaster. It was night, and there was heavy snow, remember? Callum, the rider, really couldn't see who took the mochila. They even gave him a fresh horse and a pouch to take back with him."

Jack drummed his fingers on the table. Piece by piece, he seemed to take in Lexie's explanation. "There *was* a big snowstorm that night," he said. "You couldn't see two feet in front of you."

"The trouble is," Billy said, "once they had the ring, they didn't know what to do with it."

"Not many rich ladies out here," Jack agreed. "Or ladies with rich husbands to buy them treasures like this."

Pike's scowl deepened. "Not in this God-forsaken country!" he muttered. "Got to sell it to the coyotes!"

"So do you see? That Pony rider didn't steal anything!" Lexie burst out. "They should never have accused him."

Finally, Jack turned on Pike. "You didn't just steal a ring," he told Pike fiercely. "You hurt the reputation of the Pony Express!"

"That's right," Billy said, nodding. "The Pony Express promises to get the mail through on time."

"And you were ready to let an innocent man go to the gallows!" Jack added. "A poor fellow that was trying to do his job."

Pike said nothing. He didn't look remorseful or ashamed, only angry.

"I know that innocent man," Lexie said into the silence. "His name is Callum McDonald."

"I'll see to it that they know his name from one end of the trail to the other," Jack declared, with a fire in his eyes. "I'll tell every rider who comes in and have him pass the word along. Callum McDonald was set up. We've got the fellow that stole from the Pony Express, and Callum McDonald is innocent! The company sure is grateful to you, Alex, for setting this right. People were beginning to talk about the reliability of our services."

Billy Cates and Jack Corley bound Pike's hands behind him and tied his feet so that he couldn't run off. Now that Jack understood the full story, his mind clamped down on one idea—Pike and Driscoll would pay for their evil deeds. "The division superintendent is due in tomorrow," he said. "He can take this fellow off my hands and see that justice is done."

"Maybe he can scare up a posse too and go after the other one," Billy added. "He's still prowling around somewhere."

"They'll get him," Jack said confidently. "Nobody who attacks the Pony Express is going to get away with it."

"What will happen to the ring?" Lexie asked. "Will you give it to the superintendent?"

Jack scratched his head, pondering. The rain had dwindled to a soft drumming on the roof, and thunder rumbled in the distance. "The ring should have been delivered six months ago," Jack said finally. "It ought to go today, as soon as the westbound rider comes in."

"I need to be off with the eastbound mail," Billy said. "Pike has put me two hours behind schedule."

"Put on some dry things first," Jack said. "You won't be any good to the Pony if you catch pneumonia." He went to a cupboard in the corner. "I've got something in here for you, too," he told Lexie over his shoulder. He said nothing to Pike, who sat grimly silent in his rain-soaked clothes.

After rummaging for a few moments, Jack handed Billy and Lexie each a fresh pair of britches and a clean, dry shirt.

Oh, no! Lexie thought. She took the clothes and glanced desperately around her. The station was tiny; it had only one room. She couldn't change her clothes here, in front of these three men! She couldn't!

Billy knew her secret. Perhaps he could rescue her somehow. Lexie cast him a look of appeal. He hesitated and pointed to the door. But she couldn't step outside to change into dry clothes under the dripping trees. She'd give herself away for sure!

Billy didn't waste any more time. In seconds he shucked off his wet clothes and slipped into the dry ones that Jack had provided. Lexie shifted from one foot to the other. She began to shiver in her wet shirt and britches. She longed to put on the dry clothes draped over her arm, but it seemed utterly impossible.

"Well?" Jack asked with a shade of annoyance. "What are you waiting for?"

"Nothing . . ." She looked longingly at the door. Maybe she could dash outside and change behind the station. It would only take a moment . . .

"Are you shy?" Jack asked. "You're acting like a modest girl!"

Pike snickered. "Maybe he is a she!" he sneered. "Maybe she wants to wear that ring herself!"

Confused, Jack looked back and forth from Pike to Lexie.

Pike's hands were tied, but nothing stopped his mouth. He continued, "Listen to how the little runt talks! She's got a girly voice! What's your name, honey? Mary? Pearl? Sarah Jane?"

"His name is Alex," Billy broke in, but Jack didn't seem to hear him. He gave Lexie a long, searching look that made her shiver harder than ever.

"I had a hunch something wasn't right," Jack said slowly, "but I couldn't put my finger on it. You *are* a girl, aren't you?"

It wasn't a question; it was a statement of fact. "No," Lexie stammered. "I'm . . . I'm—"

Pike gave a loud guffaw. "Look at her blush!" he cried. "What more proof do you need?"

Lexie tried to cover her face with her hands. *No!* she thought in confusion. *A boy would never do that.* She lowered her hands and stood up straight and proud.

"Tell me the truth," Jack said. "Are you traveling in disguise?"

"Yes," Lexie said quietly. "I'm . . . a girl. My name is Lexie McDonald. I'm Callum McDonald's sister."

✶ Chapter Twelve ✶

Pike narrowed his eyes. "You—*you're* that stupid rider's sister?" he asked, incredulous.

"Yes, she is," Billy said. "And she's the one who's brought you in. You can think about that while you wait for the law to get here. Now keep your mouth shut."

Pike sat there, fuming.

Then Billy turned to Lexie. "The mail has to go through on time. I've got to get riding again."

She knew he was anxious to resume his eastward journey, but he took the time to share a few final moments with her.

Saying good-bye to Billy was harder than Lexie could have imagined. They stood together in the doorway, and Billy clasped her hand between both of his. "I sent your message to Callum," he said in a low voice. "He knows you're on the way. Take care of yourself."

"Thank you," she said. "It's still a long way to Salt Lake City."

"You'll make it," Billy assured her. "You've got the worst part behind you!"

"I sure hope so!" Lexie said with a laugh.

"I'll be looking for Driscoll's horse on my way back," Billy said. "If he broke a leg—well, I have my pistol."

Lexie shuddered. She knew what he meant. There was no hope for a horse with a broken leg. It had to be given a swift and painless death.

"Don't worry about Jack," Billy went on. "He won't tell anybody your secret."

"And Pike probably won't want everyone to know he was brought in by a girl," Lexie said.

"You'll find Callum," Billy said after a moment. "I know you will."

With that, Billy checked his mochila and mounted

his horse. With a burst of speed, he headed down the trail. Lexie waved until he disappeared.

Now that her secret was out, Lexie walked around behind the station and put on her dry clothes in complete privacy. From the pocket of Callum's sopping britches she drew the last of her money, her father's handkerchief, and her mother's necklace of blue glass beads. Carefully, she slipped them all into the pocket of her fresh britches.

"A girl," Jack Corley murmured when she went inside again. "I don't think a girl has ever set foot in this cabin before."

"I can't stay long," Lexie said. "As soon as my horse, Cougar, has had a rest, I have to be going to find my brother."

"I can't send you off by yourself!" Jack protested. "It's dangerous out there!"

"I know," Lexie said, gesturing toward Pike. "I can take care of myself."

Jack looked at Pike, and finally the story of everything she'd done since she left Willow Springs must have sunk in.

Jack shrugged, defeated. He turned his attention to getting the ring ready for the westbound rider. He found some brown paper and twine and rewrapped the precious package. Carefully, Lexie copied the address. With satisfaction, she read it aloud: "Forty-six Lombard Street, San Francisco, California." In just a few more days the gold miner's bride would have her diamond, and the world would know that Callum McDonald was an innocent man.

"Did I hear a horn?" Jack asked, cocking his head. He went to the door and peered out. In a few moments he stepped back inside. "Must have been the wind," he said, disappointed. "Tommy Ranahan is an hour overdue."

"Is he the rider heading west?" Lexie asked.

"That's him. Little red-haired fellow. Not like him to be late."

Jack ladled out two bowls of soup, and they sat down to eat. "Later for you," he told Pike. "I'll untie your hands and let you have a meal, long as I've got a gun on you."

Lexie hadn't known she was so hungry. The soup was a concoction of beans, meat scraps, and some leafy vegetable that she didn't recognize. She savored each heavenly spoonful. She hadn't eaten since Three Crossings!

Again Jack Corley went to look outside. Once more he returned, shaking his head with concern. "It isn't like Tommy to fall behind schedule," he said. "The mail has to keep moving!"

"He might have run into Driscoll," Lexie said, troubled.

"Tommy's been around. He can handle it," Jack said, trying to reassure them both. It didn't do much good. Lexie observed that he kept shaking his head and glancing at the waiting package.

On a shelf Lexie noticed an empty mochila. It looked oddly lifeless with nothing inside to give it form. A wonderful, tantalizing thought floated into her mind. "If Tommy Ranahan doesn't come pretty soon," she ventured, "maybe I could take the ring myself?"

"The company wouldn't allow that!" Jack said sternly. "I'm only permitted to hand the mail to an official Pony Express rider."

"Of course," said Lexie. "But the company doesn't like the mail to be late either. And this ring, like you said—it's six months late already."

"True enough," Jack said. "If you were a boy, maybe. But you—no, I'm sorry."

"I'm a girl, but I'm not afraid of much," she

pointed out. "I can take care of myself on the trail."

Jack tugged at his beard. Lexie tried to contain her impatience as her idea made its way into his mind. If only he would say yes! If only, just once, she could carry the mail like a real Pony rider!

"Suppose you take the ring," Jack pondered, "and then Tommy comes in after all?"

"He can take a fresh horse and catch up with me," Lexie pointed out. "I'll ride Cougar. You can hold the fresh horse for Tommy."

Jack nodded, pleased. But soon another worry assailed him. "The company makes all the riders take the pledge," he fretted. "They only trust the mail to honest, clean-living young men."

"You know I'm trustworthy!" Lexie exclaimed. "I handed the ring over, didn't I?"

"Well, yes," Jack admitted. "You're honest. I can't argue with that."

Lexie's eagerness got the better of her. "Let me take the ring," she said, leaning forward with excitement. "Please?"

"Tommy's not here, and the package has to go through," Jack mused, weighing the situation piece by piece. "Yes, I suppose you can carry it yourself."

Lexie didn't give him time to change his mind. She picked up the empty mochila, slipped the package into one of the pouches, and headed for the door.

"Just a minute!" Jack called. "I need to give you a couple of things before you go."

From a shelf in the corner he took a pistol and a long brass horn. Gravely, he handed them to Lexie. "When you get close to Green River Station, blow the horn as a signal," he explained. "And the pistol—I guess you know what that's for."

"I guess I do," she said, laughing. "I hope I won't need it, though. I've had enough excitement for a while."

From the holster in her belt, Lexie removed the battered pistol that she'd taken from the cave and replaced it with the Pony gun. It was a beautiful pistol, and Lexie was proud to carry it.

Out in the corral she prepared Cougar for the next leg of their journey and placed the mochila over his saddle. Lexie mounted and tied the horn behind her, as she had seen Pony riders do so many times back at Willow Springs.

"Just follow the trail," Jack told her. "Green River's the next station."

Suppose Tommy Ranahan doesn't catch up with us?

Lexie wondered. There would be no one to carry the mochila west from Green River. How much farther could Cougar travel without a long rest? She decided it would be wise not to raise the question. She had already given Jack more than enough to handle.

"We're off!" she cried, waving good-bye. "Come on, Cougar! We've got to carry the mail!"

Perhaps Cougar had enjoyed a good long rest last night, while Lexie was being held captive in the cave. He didn't seem tired, despite his race with the outlaws. The trail out to Green River Station was steep, but he climbed at a smooth, steady trot. When they reached a plateau, he broke into a canter, only to slow down when the trail grew steep again.

They reached the top of a rocky outcropping, with the peak of a mountain rising sheer above them. Ahead the trail threaded between two massive granite boulders, each the size of a small house. Lexie eyed the trail warily. She had good reason to mistrust narrow passages, she told herself. She wished she could find a more open route, but there seemed to be no other way. At least the treeless rocks offered no hiding places for skulking bandits, she assured herself. And it was broad daylight. She was perfectly safe.

Lexie urged Cougar forward, and he set off confidently. The boulders pressed in on both sides, and the air felt tight and close. The sun shone brightly, as though the sky had forgotten the storm of an hour ago. *There is nothing to be afraid of*, Lexie repeated to herself. *Nothing to be afraid of. Nothing—*

She felt Cougar stiffen, even before she saw him lay his ears flat against his neck. He lifted his head, nostrils flaring, to read the messages in the air. Lexie scanned the walls of the passage for warning signs. Something was wrong, and Cougar knew it.

Suddenly, above her, Lexie glimpsed a flicker of movement on an overhanging ledge of rock. Her heart pounding, she stared, trying to discern a living form. A pair of cold yellow eyes stared back. For the briefest instant she saw a tawny head, whiskers fanned beside snarling jaws. Then, with a terrible scream, the sinewy body of a giant cat sprang free of the rock and hurtled toward them.

Cougar plunged forward, trying vainly to outrun his attacker. Lexie felt a sickening jolt as the cat landed behind her. She heard its grating growl and felt its breath hot on the back of her neck. Then Cougar reared high on his hind legs. He leaped and twisted, desperate to fling the cat from his back. The cat clung tightly, but Lexie sailed through the air and crashed full-length to the ground. She heard Cougar scream in terror and rage and saw the cat looming above her. Then the world melted away, and she glided down a long slide into unconsciousness.

✳ Chapter Thirteen ✳

Her head throbbed. Lexie shifted restlessly, as though she might move away from the pain, but there was no escape. Something rustled softly whenever she moved, like the whisper of pine boughs. She stretched her arms, trying to read her surroundings, and heard the rustling again. She seemed to be lying on a blanket spread over something soft and springy. Voices murmured nearby, a man's and a woman's, hovering somewhere in the air above her. They were gentle and comforting, and the pain began to ease. The man's voice was strangely familiar. *Maybe I'm dreaming*, Lexie thought. It was a lovely dream, and she didn't want to wake up. She kept her eyes closed, fighting to hold the dream in place.

The sweet dream faded, and a parade of ragged images took its place. Suddenly, she and Cougar were galloping down a steep trail. Then, just as suddenly, she was alone, crouched in a cave and hiding from an enemy. Next she was a little girl back in the village of her childhood, and someone was calling her. Did she know that voice? Was it Mama?

Lexie opened her eyes. A woman leaned over her, speaking softly. Her high cheekbones and bronze complexion recalled a time long ago, when Lexie and Callum lived with Papa and Mama and all the people of the village. To her own amazement, Lexie heard herself utter words that she thought she had forgotten, the words of a greeting in the Inuna-Ina tongue.

"We were looking for you," the woman answered in the same language. She said more words, but Lexie couldn't understand. Smiling kindly, the woman turned and called softly to someone else.

A tall, slim figure emerged from the shadows. "Lexie," said a voice she had known all her life. "You're finally awake!"

Lexie sat bolt upright, forgetting the vague pounding in her head. "Callum?" she asked in wonder. "Is it really you?"

"Yes, it's me—your brother." Callum bent toward her and held out his hand. She clasped it tightly, and he helped her to her feet. His smile was dignified, quiet, and somehow very Indian. Lexie knew no such restraint. She flung herself into her brother's arms with joyful abandon. Callum's dignity gave way, and he swung her around in delight as if she was still a little girl.

But Lexie's joy was tinged with sadness. When they were finally calm enough to speak, she said, "I have terrible news."

Callum nodded. "About Papa," he said. "I know."

"You got Billy's message?" Lexie asked.

"He passed it down the line," Callum said. "A couple of the other riders knew how to find me. They made sure I heard what happened."

Lexie was still reeling with the shock of seeing him. "I thought you were in Salt Lake City!" she exclaimed. "That's where I was heading."

"I was there for two months," Callum told her. "In April I came back to Wyoming and met up with some of our mama's people. It's a long story. But when I got another message from Billy that you were following the Pony trail, with your hair cut short, I set out with Margaret," he said, gesturing toward the woman, "and we headed east along the trail to meet you."

Margaret had been standing a little apart, listening quietly. Now Callum turned to her. "Margaret," he said, "this is my sister, Lexie. Lexie, this is Margaret 'Singing Reed,' my wife."

"Your wife!" Lexie cried. "When did you get married?"

"In June, in an Arapaho ceremony in the Absarokas," he said, smiling. "We stay in this cabin when we're not up on the range. I'm becoming a horse trader," he added proudly. "I catch mustangs and tame them to sell, and Margaret helps me.

"You can come with us," Margaret said. "Callum says you're good with horses."

At the thought of horses, Lexie felt a wrench of fear. Where was Cougar? How could she forget him, even for a moment? The last time she'd seen him he was trying to throw the mountain lion—the giant cat that snarled above her. What had happened? How had she survived, and where was Cougar now?

"Callum," she asked urgently, "where's Cougar?"

As soon as she'd asked the question, Lexie realized that she might not want to know the answer.

Callum said quietly, "I didn't see him, Lexie, but there was a lot of blood."

"How far is it?" Lexie demanded. "We've got to go back there! We've got to find him!"

Callum hesitated. "It's a long ride," he said. "Maybe you should wait till you feel better."

"I'm fine," she insisted. "Cougar might be hurt. He might need me! We can't lose any more time!"

Callum and Margaret looked at each other. She said something to him in Inuna-Ina.

"She thinks we should go," Callum translated. "She's afraid you'll get lost in the dreamworld again, from sadness, if we say no."

"I don't know what happened for sure," Lexie told them, "but I think Cougar saved my life. I have to try to save his."

Chapter Fourteen

Since they had only two horses between them, Margaret stayed behind at the cabin. Callum rode his bay gelding, Ranger, and Lexie rode Cornflower, Margaret's pinto mare. As they hurried back, Lexie told Callum about the attack by the mountain lion. "A horse can kill a lion with his hooves," Callum said. "But a lion has his teeth and claws. A lion can kill a horse, too."

The image of Cougar fighting the lion flashed into Lexie's mind. *We've got to hurry!* cried the voice inside her head. Already they might be too late.

Maybe Cornflower was nervous with an unfamiliar

rider, or maybe it was just her nature to be skittish. She shied when a meadowlark fluttered up from the underbrush. When an overhanging branch tickled her ears, she tried to veer off the trail. Lexie struggled to hold her on a steady course, while the voice in her head kept urging her to hurry.

At last they approached the passage between the boulders. Dismounting, they tethered the horses and began to search for signs. They moved in slow, careful circles, their eyes fastened on the ground. Lexie saw instantly where the pine needles were trampled and the earth was gouged by frantic hooves. Clearly, a deadly battle had taken place here a very short time ago. But who had won—and who had lost?

"There!" Callum whispered, pointing. "Blood."

Lexie bent and studied the spots of crimson staining the pine needles. *Am I looking at Cougar's blood*, she wondered with a shudder, *or the blood of the cat that had tried to kill him?*

There were actually two bloody trails, they discovered, crossing and recrossing one another over a pine-dotted plateau. One trail must lead to Cougar and the other to the mountain lion.

At the edge of the plateau the blood spots became

scattered and harder to follow. They disappeared in a tumble of rocks a few feet below. After scouting along the rim, Lexie discovered a series of rocks that descended like natural steps.

As they climbed down, Lexie braced herself to find the worst. She imagined Cougar dead, torn to pieces by the mountain lion's claws. Even if he was still alive, he might be beyond saving. She remembered Driscoll's horse back on the trail and how Billy Cates promised to end its agony. She was still wearing the pistol that Jack Corley had given her. She would hand it to Callum if Cougar was beyond any other help. Callum would do what had to be done.

About 20 feet down they reached a ledge that was around three feet wide. Stopping to catch her breath, Lexie noticed a big smear of blood on the stone. She crouched down to examine it more closely. "Look!" she cried. "Here's another trail of spots, see?"

"It's the cat," Callum said. "See, it left tracks here. We've got to be careful."

The tracks were bloody scrawls in the dirt, large round paws and a dragging tail. It appeared that the mountain lion had been clawing its way forward, too badly injured to stand.

The spots led from rock to rock, sometimes following a jutting shelf, sometimes traveling downward. At last, half hidden by a tangle of bushes, Lexie saw a tawny form. It was the mountain lion, and in the first instant she knew that it was dead.

"It's amazing it managed to crawl this far," Callum said. "Look at its head."

Even in death, the cat's body was sinewy and strangely graceful. But above the right ear, pieces of splintered bone showed through the ragged, bloody pelt. Cougar's thrashing hooves had given the creature a deathblow.

Lexie stroked the cat's lean flank with a cautious hand. "It's beautiful!" she breathed. "How could anything so beautiful be so dangerous?"

"What's that?" Callum cried. "Over there—look!" Tucked between two rocks lay the horn that Jack Corley had given Lexie as a symbol of the Pony Express.

Callum stared at it in amazement. "Why— " he began.

"I was carrying the mail," she said quickly. "I can't explain it now. Cougar must be nearby."

In a haze of fear and hope Lexie clambered down the rocks, her eyes searching for the crimson splotches that marked Cougar's trail. Suddenly, she heard a low, gasping moan. She had never before heard a horse utter such a sound, but she knew that she had found Cougar at last.

He lay on his side, his legs outstretched, his coat matted with blood. His eyes were closed. For a dizzying moment she was certain that the moan had been his last gasp of life. Then she saw the slight lifting of his side as he drew a breath, and her heart gave a lurch of hope.

She went to him slowly, not wanting to frighten him. Kneeling by his side, she rested her hand on his shoulder. "Cougar," she whispered. "Can you hear me? It's Lexie! Cougar, open your eyes!"

Cougar didn't stir. Only the rise and fall of his side told her that he was still alive. "He's got some pretty bad gashes from the lion's claws," Callum said, examining him swiftly. "But it looks like none of his legs are broken."

"It seems like he's in shock," Lexie said fearfully.

Callum nodded. "I've seen it in mustangs up in the mountains," he said. "They go through something really bad, like being captured or hurt, and they just give up. He's trying to let go of the world."

Lexie remembered her own terrible sense of helplessness when Pike and Driscoll loaded her onto their horse. She had almost given up hope, frozen like a terrified rabbit. She couldn't let that happen to Cougar.

Every fiber of her being focused on sending Cougar a message. "You're going to be all right," she murmured. "Open your eyes now. You're safe. Just open your eyes."

For a few moments nothing happened. Then a quiver passed through Cougar's body. He opened his eyes and lifted his head to look at her.

Lexie felt a brief surge of relief, but she knew that Cougar was still in peril. His gaze was dull with pain and misery. He clung to life by only the finest thread. Lexie choked back her tears and went on coaxing him with her voice. "Yes," she said, "that's right. Keep your eyes open. Now you need to get up. Come on—try to get up on your feet."

Bit by bit, with bursts of movement between long pauses, Cougar gathered his legs beneath him. His breath came in short, harsh rasps as he struggled to lift his body from the ground. At last, shuddering with the effort, he heaved himself onto his feet. His eyes looked brighter now. He cocked his ears and looked around him with an air of surprise, as though he had been away for a long time.

"The lion is dead," Lexie told him. "You killed it,

Cougar—and you survived!" She wondered if Cougar carried a distant memory of the cat that had killed his mother. Maybe he had fought so fiercely from some deep recognition of his enemy.

"The mochila!" Lexie exclaimed. "He still has the mochila on his back."

As Callum watched, Lexie unfastened the pouch and slipped her hand inside. Slowly, she drew out the package that she and Jack had wrapped with such painstaking care. "Callum!" she breathed. "We have the ring! Look!"

Mystified, Callum took the package and read the San Francisco address. "What does this mean?" he asked, looking up.

Lexie said, "It means that you don't have to hide anymore. I found the men who robbed the Pony. Your name is clear!"

"I don't understand," Callum said. He handed the package back to Lexie as if it had burned his fingers.

"The ring is in this package," Lexie told him. "I was captured by the same bandits who robbed you. I found it in their cave, and after I escaped I brought it to Big Sandy and told Jack Corley everything. Then he let me take it on to the next station, but we never made it."

Callum lifted his hand, waving her to a halt. "Bandits?" he repeated. "I never saw any bandits. I turned over my mochila to the stationmaster."

"That's what they wanted you to think," Lexie explained. "They made a lean-to *look* like a station. The man you thought was the stationmaster was really an outlaw. It was all a trick so that they could get their hands on the ring."

"And you got it back!" Callum said in awe. "Oh, Lexie! What an amazing sister you are! How did you do it?"

"Because I had to," Lexie said quietly. "So many times, riding along on the trail, I thought about Papa. I thought how he died without seeing you again, worrying that you'd be caught and hanged, and I wished I could find a way to clear your name. So, once I learned that Pike and Driscoll had the ring, I knew I had to escape—for your sake and for Papa's, too."

"You've done it for all of us," Callum said. "Now I can deliver the ring to Green River. I can bring it in myself."

Searching out the smoothest footing, Lexie led Cougar back up to the plateau. "It's only three miles to the station," Callum said. "We'll take it slowly, but we'll get there."

"I'll walk by Cougar's head," Lexie said. "I need to

tend to his wounds as soon as I can."

"Margaret will help you when we get back to the cabin," said Callum. "She's good at doctoring the horses."

"Maybe she'll teach me," Lexie said. "And . . . I'd like to learn our language again too."

Callum smiled. "There's a loft that can be your room and a nice corral for Cougar. I think you'll like it—if you want to stay."

"I'll love it," Lexie assured him. "I feel like I'm finally coming home!"

Behind them they heard the pounding of hooves. A rider on a galloping horse swept toward them, waving jauntily as he passed. "It's the westbound rider!" Lexie cried. "We can give him the mochila when we get to Green River."

Cougar whinnied, gazing after the Pony rider as if he longed to run and catch up.

"He's a tough little horse," Callum said. "It looks like you've brought him back from the edge."

"We're a team," Lexie told him, smiling. "Cougar and I can take on anything when we're together."

* * *

*To whet your appetite for another thrilling
adventure in the* Saddles, Stars, & Stripes *series,
read on for the opening chapter of*
Chance of a Lifetime.

★ SADDLES, STARS, & STRIPES ★

CHANCE OF A LIFETIME

DEBORAH KENT

MISSISSIPPI, 1863
AND THE CIVIL WAR RAGES ALL AROUND . . .

Returning home from a visit with her relatives, 14-year-old Jacquetta May Logan finds her family's plantation commandeered by the Union army. Alone in enemy territory with only Chance, her beloved bay gelding, for company, Jacquetta forges an unexpected friendship with a brave slave girl named Peace. Together, they devise a daring plan to rescue her family's Morgan horses and lead them to safety across the Mississippi river. But danger lurks at every step of the way . . .

✶ Chapter One ✶

Slowly, reluctantly, Jacquetta May Logan walked from the barn back to the house. The July heat felt dense, like a thick cloud she had to push aside with every step. It had been deliciously cool in the woods, where the leaves and branches filtered out the rays of the sun. She'd ridden along a wide, shady trail on her bay gelding, Chance, breathing in the fresh air and grateful for half an hour away from the sewing room. If only she could have gone on riding till sundown, she thought. Aunt Clem would never allow it, of course. There was too much work to be done.

Sighing, Jacquetta slipped into the house through the side door. She crossed the hall and headed for the drawing room, where the sewing table waited, heaped with blue homespun ready to be made into clothes for the family at Brookmoor.

Aunt Clem was there to greet her. "Jacquetta May!" she exclaimed. "Where have you been?"

"I went for a ride—just a quick one," she said. "I've finished the bodice."

Aunt Clem frowned. "I see you have," she said, holding up Jacquetta's work. "If you hadn't been in such a hurry, you'd have remembered the sleeves."

Jacquetta felt her face flush. "I'm sorry," she said. "I'll do them now."

From the far end of the table Cousin Mattie offered a smile of sympathy. Jacquetta smiled back as she dropped into her seat. Dainty, golden-haired Mattie never slipped away from her work, Jacquetta thought, no matter how tedious the task or stifling the room. Mattie's thread never tangled or broke. Her hems were always beautifully straight, and her seams were almost invisible. Her needle darted in and out, in and out, leaving a chain of perfect little stitches in its trail. It hurt Jacquetta's head just to watch her.

Jacquetta found her needle where she had stuck it into a scrap of cloth. With a will of its own, the thread twisted into a knot as she tried to slip the end through the needle's eye. Aunt Clem watched over her shoulder. "You're fourteen, aren't you?" she asked. "By fourteen, sewing should come as natural as breathing."

Jacquetta thought of the rake-thin, scowling sewing teacher at Miss Woodworth's Seminary for Young Ladies, the boarding school she had attended in Virginia. "At Miss Woodworth's they said I'll never be a seamstress," she admitted.

"What did they teach you then?" Aunt Clem wanted to know.

"French," Jacquetta said with a little shudder. "Elocution—reciting poetry and making speeches. And deportment. Deportment every day." She'd spent endless hours walking with books balanced on her head in order to keep her posture straight, practicing sitting and rising in her swirling skirts, and learning how and when to curtsy.

Aunt Clem shook her head. "All well and good," she said, "if these were ordinary times."

Jacquetta took up the panels of the bodice and pinned on the missing sleeves. If she wanted to take Chance out for a longer ride today, she'd have to finish a presentable piece of work. She'd do whatever she had to do for a few hours of freedom!

Aunt Clem took up her own sewing again to set the right example. "We all have to work together," she declared, seated at the head of the table. "We're not just sewing for ourselves, remember. We're sewing for the Cause of the South!"

Jacquetta recognized the patient, resigned bow of Mattie's shoulders. After 17 years on this earth Mattie knew her mother pretty well. They were in for a lecture, and it might go on for hours.

"You girls should be proud of your heritage," Aunt Clem began, starting slowly, like a fiddler tuning up at a dance. "You come from the best stock in Mississippi. The Logans came out from Virginia when your grandfather was a little boy. They trace back to the best Virginia families too. The Washingtons and the Madisons are some of your own kin, don't forget that."

Whenever Aunt Clem started to talk about fine stock, Jacquetta couldn't help thinking about horses. The beautiful Morgans her father raised at Green Haven had a heritage to be proud of. Her papa had bought the stallion Samoset on a trip to New England, along with a string of Morgan mares. That had been back in 1849, the year Jacquetta was born. Now the Green Haven line was famous all over the South. You could tell well-bred horses by the way they held their heads high, by the grace and power of their movements. You couldn't miss their quick intelligence and eagerness to learn. Were there signs like that in people? Jacquetta wondered. If you lined up folks from three Mississippi families, could a stranger spot the Logans on account of their fine stock?

"That's why we're fighting this dreadful war," Aunt Clem went on, her voice rising. "The Yankees have no respect for our Southern heritage. They don't understand our way of life. And they think they can beat us." She struck the bell that stood beside her on the table and continued, "They think they can starve us out by blockading our ports. We can't import supplies, we can't sell our cotton, so they think they've got us in a corner. Well, they haven't got us. We'll make uniforms for our boys in the army. We'll make homespun clothes for ourselves. Every stitch we sew is an act of patriotism."

A black servant girl from the kitchen opened the door. "Yes'm?" she asked.

"Bring us some lemonade and some of Ella's fresh tarts," Aunt Clem told her. As the girl disappeared, she resumed, "We've all got to do our part. Even if it means doing chores we don't enjoy, we've got to pitch in for the Cause." Jacquetta struggled with her needle as Aunt Clem's words rattled around her. If you measured loyalty by how well a person did chores, she reflected, then she was a traitor to the Confederacy.

※

Aunt Clem's lecture finally ended when the servant girl came back with the tray. Sewing forgotten, Aunt Clem, Jacquetta, and Mattie moved onto the veranda for their well-earned refreshments. The spreading magnolia trees created a semblance of shade. Jacquetta breathed in the scent of honeysuckle and gazed out across the rolling fields. Half a dozen of Uncle Silas' Jersey cows grazed quietly in the distance, down near the brook that edged the woods.

"Well, Jacquetta," Aunt Clem said, passing the plate of tarts, "you've been here a week now, haven't you? It's so sweet of your mama to loan you to us."

"Thank you, ma'am," Jacquetta said politely. "It's lovely to be here." "Loan" was an apt word to describe the situation, she mused. Mattie had been unbearably lonely here at Brookmoor, and Aunt Clem had asked Jacquetta to come for an extended visit. Jacquetta was good company for Mattie, even though Mattie was three years older.

The tarts were delicious, each baked in a crisp golden shell and still warm from the oven. Jacquetta loved the contrast between the sweet pastries and the tangy lemonade. She leaned back in her wicker chair and listened to the joyful song of a mockingbird. It was so peaceful here at Brookmoor. She could almost forget about the men off fighting and the Yankees with their cannons and cavalry. She could pretend they were still living back in the days before the war, when everyone was safe.

But she couldn't pretend the war away. If it wasn't for the war, her brothers, Adam and Marcus, would still be home at Green Haven. She never stopped worrying about them. Had any news come? Was Mama crying again, while she, Jacquetta, munched tarts on Aunt Clem's veranda? It wasn't right for her to be away at Brookmoor, where she didn't know if some new trouble had taken hold of her family at this very minute. Somehow the more she enjoyed her visit, the more she felt the need to go home again.

Away from the sewing table, Aunt Clem's natural warmth emerged. "Whatever happens, we've got to look for the silver lining," Aunt Clem remarked. "You're a silver lining for us in this war, Jacquetta May."

"Thank you," she said. "It's sweet of you to say so." After a moment she added, "Another silver lining is coming home from Virginia. The war let me get away from Miss Woodworth's."

It had felt like a miracle in February when Papa sent for her to come home, right in the middle of the semester. It was the answer to her prayers. There was too much fighting in Virginia, Papa wrote. It wasn't safe for her to be so far away. Not that it was any safer in Mississippi, now that the Yankees had Vicksburg under siege. Sometimes they could hear the distant roar of cannon fire as they sat on the veranda at Green Haven. That was the real reason Papa had lent her to Aunt Clem now. He thought Green Haven was becoming too dangerous for his only daughter. Brookmoor was ten miles south and farther inland from the Mississippi river. The noise of cannons didn't reach them here.

Jacquetta had been overjoyed to leave Miss Woodworth's, to turn her back on French verbs and elocution—and most of all on deportment class. Sometimes Miss Woodworth's voice still chimed inside her head: "Say 'Yes, ma'am' and 'No, ma'am.'" "Curtsy when you leave the room." "Sit up straight, Jacquetta! A lady always sits with her ankles together." Now, on Aunt Clem's veranda, she slid down in her chair and defiantly sprawled her legs before her so that her ankles showed plainly beneath the edge of her skirts.

Hooves clattered on the drive, and the wagon rolled into view, with Uncle Silas perched on the seat. They hadn't expected him back from town until evening, bringing news and whatever supplies he could bargain for. He couldn't have gotten much business done in so short a time. Aunt Clem would start to scold and Uncle Silas would protest, and it all meant an end to these fragile moments of peace on the veranda.

Uncle Silas drew the wagon to a stop and climbed down slowly. Jacquetta saw that his hat was gone, and his hand trembled as he passed the reins to one of the stable boys. The boy began to unhitch the horses, a matching pair of black geldings named Jeff and Davis. Uncle Silas prized his team. He said President Jefferson Davis would be proud to know that such fine horses were named in his honor.

*

"Clementine!" Uncle Silas called. His voice cracked, and he tottered on his feet.

Aunt Clem sprang down from the veranda and rushed to meet him. "What's wrong, Silas?" she demanded. "What happened?"

"Grant's taken Vicksburg," he answered. "It's finished. They say in town—" He stopped, struggling for words. "They say blood ran in the streets. Like a river. A river of blood."

For a long, stunned moment no one spoke. Then Aunt Clem began to cry. She and Uncle Silas stood with their arms around each other, swaying together in grief. Mattie reached for Jacquetta's hand. Mattie was crying too, but Jacquetta felt too dazed even for tears. Marcus and Adam were in Vicksburg. Were they all right? Had Mama and Papa heard any news about them? And if Vicksburg was in the hands of the Yankees, what would happen to Green Haven, only seven miles away?

That night Ella, the cook, served up a generous dinner of fried chicken and sweet potatoes, but no one took more than a few bites. Jacquetta looked desperately from her aunt to her uncle, longing for them to assure her that everything would be all right. Their faces were haggard with pain and dread. They gave no comfort, only a sense of foreboding that she had never known before. She listened in horror as the dreadful possibilities unfolded before her.

"What's to stop them now?" Aunt Clem asked. "They'll burn our houses! Trample our crops and leave us all to starve!"

"Do you really think they'll come here, to Brookmoor?" Mattie asked.

"From Vicksburg they'll have the run of the country," Uncle Silas said grimly. "I'll burn my cotton before I let the Yankees get their hands on it!"

Mattie began to cry again. "We'll all be

murdered! I hear they kill Rebel babies! They stick them on pitchforks!"

Aunt Clem looked furtively around the dining room and lowered her voice. "What worries me—they might stir up the Negroes. Get our own servants to turn against us."

"Servants" was the word genteel people used when they spoke about slaves, Jacquetta thought. They were fighting this terrible war over slavery, yet most of the people she knew didn't even like to use the word.

All of the windows were open, but it felt as if there wasn't enough air in the room. Jacquetta longed to escape. She filled her mind with a picture that made her happy. She was back at Green Haven, and none of this was happening. The faces of her brothers floated before her. She heard Adam's teasing voice: "Go on, Jacquie! I dare you to jump over the pasture fence!" She brought

Chance to a steady canter, and then they were up and over in a glide so smooth that she hardly felt the ground as they landed on the other side.

Chance had been a present for Jacquetta's 12th birthday. Back then he was a frolicking two-year-old colt who'd never felt a saddle on his back. Jacquetta used to bring treats for him out in the field—carrots and sugar lumps and slices of apples. She taught Chance to come when she whistled, like a big, friendly dog. Papa and Adam helped Jacquetta train him on the saddle. The first time Marcus saw her ride the frisky bay gelding he clapped his hands and said she was born for the saddle.

The bright pictures faded away. Where was Adam now? He'd volunteered last October, as soon as he turned 16. Marcus, two years older, had already been in uniform for a year. Her mind formed a hideous question, and she

＊

couldn't push it away. Had their blood flowed
with that river in the streets of Vicksburg? She
tried to imagine what they must have seen and
heard—the roar of cannons, the choking clouds
of smoke, the screams of men and horses dying
in agony.

"I'm going back to the Mississippi Volunteers,"
Uncle Silas declared. "They've got to take
me now."

"You can't!" Aunt Clem cried. "We need you
here! Who's going to protect me and the girls?"

Uncle Silas seemed to expand in his chair at the
head of the table. "The Mississippi Volunteers will
defend our women and children," he promised.
"Before the Yankees touch a blade of grass at
Brookmoor, they'll have to contend with us."

At 61, Uncle Silas was almost 20 years older
than Aunt Clem, but that hadn't stopped him
from trying to enlist when the war broke out

two years ago, back in 1861. The recruiting officer had called him "Grandpap" and sent him home, angry and ashamed. It would be different this time, Jacquetta thought. They'd probably take any man who could hold a rifle. Her stomach gave a sickening lurch. They might even take Papa. His bad leg had kept him out of the war so far, but the army wouldn't be particular anymore. Papa wasn't like Uncle Silas; he hadn't wanted to send the boys to fight, and he hadn't wanted to go himself. He didn't talk much about patriotism and the Cause. Jacquetta almost believed he wished that the South had never left the Union, though he wouldn't say such a thing out loud. She couldn't imagine him in uniform, limping along with his regiment, firing a gun at fellow human beings, even if they were Yankees. And suppose he was wounded! Or even worse . . .

The words tumbled out before she knew what she was going to say. "Aunt Clem—Uncle Silas—I've got to go home!"

For the first time they turned their attention to her. "Don't you even think of it!" Aunt Clem exclaimed. "The roads aren't safe. Besides, there's no one to take you. You'll stay here with us till this is over."

"I need to see my family!" she insisted. "I should be with them."

"Green Haven is even closer to Vicksburg than we are," Uncle Silas pointed out. "It doesn't make sense to take you back; it'd be like putting you right into Yankee hands."

"We're family to you," Aunt Clem said, folding Jacquetta in her arms.

Uncle Silas added, "Keep our Mattie company. Your papa will send word. Just be patient."

Jacquetta fell silent, but her mind went on

*

working. She had to get back to Green Haven somehow. She would leave tonight, even if she had to go in secret. Out in the barn Chance was waiting. She and Chance would find their way home together.